BONE
BABY

A chilling emotional suspense with a killer ending

Diane Dickson

THE BOOK FOLKS

Published by The Books Folks

London, 2017

www.thebookfolks.com

ISBN- 9781-5218-7-7852

For my family.

Chapter 1

It rained on the day of the funeral, which was right. Sun on a funeral is an abomination. The heavens should weep grey tears and mourners must turn their eyes downward in defence against the deluge. And so it was as they carried Charlotte Mary into the chapel and afterwards left her there in the silence, waiting to slide out of existence.

There were sandwiches in the pub later, drinks, and more tears and some thin laughter. It was all as it should have been.

When the small group had left, with hugs and sad smiles and shaking of heads, Lily sat in the darkened house and watched cars on the road outside throw shadows across the curtains.

At first, as she had died, in parts and pieces, starting with her physical strength and ending with the downward spiral into still breathing oblivion, the absence of Charlotte Mary hadn't really made much difference. Life had been filled with the bother of it all. The dashing back and forth, the organising and constant waiting for the phone to ring.

She had been in the hospice for weeks by then, and unreachable for days. Now though, when even the flesh and blood part of her was untouchable, there had opened a hole: a quiet, dark space. Lily sat in her own chair beside the fire. She reached over and pulled the plaid blanket from the arm of the couch, and laid it across her knees. Her eyes were fixed on the other chair, the emptiness in it.

She pushed at things circling on the edges of her mind. Things that had grown as Charlotte Mary had shrunk in her illness and Lily had begun to imagine a life on her own. There was a duty that loomed.

Very, very late in the night when even the quiet hum from the distant motorway was barely perceptible, Lily pushed the blanket to the floor, and walked through to the kitchen. She took the big old key from the top of the cupboard and fitted it into the hole in the cellar door. It turned easily. That surprised her; she expected some resistance after all this time. She curled a hand around the doorframe and groped with her finger for the switch. The noise of it was loud in her night-deadened ears, she was surprised by the brightness, had thought that the bulb would have long since ceased to function.

The smell was a familiar memory, something from the past, like laundry, like boiled onions, an old smell of damp and dirt, and stale air. As she took the first deep step, the wood creaked and she hesitated. It may be dangerous, the damp would surely have rotted the old timber, age may have wreaked havoc on the joints. If she were to tumble, head over heels down into the noisome dimness, then the problem would be solved. Maybe she would die, the end would be sudden and sharp and welcome. No-one would come for days, she could lie in the cellar and die, and wouldn't need to think anymore. She wouldn't need to act, she could avoid it all.

Fate was cruel; she reached the bottom of the stairs safely, and her feet made gentle thuds on the earth floor as she moved into the room.

At first, she had come down here often, quietly, in secret, just to be here and to take away the empty feeling. She had crept down when Charlotte Mary had been at work, or the shops, or out at another party. She had perched on the little ledge over some pipes, and sat and cried. Sometimes she had sung softly, or hummed, and always she had rocked. At first, she didn't notice the rocking but then, when the slight movement became habitual, she had let it be and swayed gently with the murmur of the song, and the distant sigh of the trees in the garden outside, above the level of this space.

She sank down onto the ledge tonight, though it was cold and damp and the chill seeped quickly through her thin funeral skirt, and brought out gooseflesh on her legs.

It was darker but she could see a little. She knew the space, had always been able to conjure it up in her mind's eye in an instant. The narrow, grimy window smeared a pale moonlit patch on the dirt. She had argued with Charlotte Mary about that space, said that the small warmth and the little light would be a benediction, but had been overruled and the earth there was old and compacted, undisturbed.

When the tears came, as she had known they would, she let them flow, and only when they became an irritation dripping across her cheeks, did she raise her arm and brush away the moisture with the cuff of her cardigan sleeve.

After many minutes, Lily rose stiffly and walked forwards. When she found the spot where the earth had been disturbed, she bent her legs and knelt on the cold ground. She laid a hand on the surface.

She hadn't intended to speak but in the event the words would have their way and assaulted the silence in a shushing whisper. "I'm sorry. I hope it's not too late. I'm so very sorry." She bent her head, closed her eyes and folded her hands in the front of her, like a Sunday School child. She murmured the Lord's Prayer, the only thing she could remember after years of denial and rejection of anything from the church of her youth.

It didn't seem enough, there must be more she could do. She turned her head back and forth.

Upstairs was a picture of Charlotte Mary which she had placed centrally on the sideboard. There was a small arrangement of flowers in front of it, a candle, the sort that was in a small glass for safety. They would do, yes, they would do very well.

Using both of her arms she pushed herself upwards and went back to the relative warmth of the kitchen and through to the living room. They hadn't even lit the candle, it had seemed too theatrical. The flowers wouldn't miss the light, they were already dying after all. She didn't like cut flowers, why would you choose to bring dying things into the house? But these had been a gift, thoughtful and given in kindness. Perfect.

Chapter 2

It was even colder now, back upstairs. Lily dragged an old jacket over her clothes and sat before her computer. For the last few days she hadn't had a chance to use the machine, and she had missed it. Though Charlotte Mary had been mocking of the hours that she spent in front of the glowing screen, it had been, for her, a thin line thrown out into the wide, virtual world. She had taken a class at the library and had loved everything about it from the start.

While Charlotte Mary had been in the hospital, over and over in the desperate battle against the various assaults of her illness, Lily had used the time alone in the house to sail around the multiple worlds that the internet had given her. She hadn't talked to many people. One or two old friends from boarding school had found her, and she had read their posts and clicked the thumbs up button under pictures of weddings, birthdays, the birth of grandchildren. Once she had sat late into the night typing tiny messages back and forth with Sophie, whose silly old husband had run away with his secretary.

She had longed to share the news with Charlotte Mary but it wasn't possible. She would have been appalled at the back and forth of personal details that Lily had been a party to. When Lily had told Sophie about Charlotte Mary's death she had offered to come to the funeral, but in the event, it hadn't worked out and really it was a relief. She wasn't strong enough to meet anyone from back then.

Now though, if she decided to sit for hours in front of the screen, sharing the little dramas that happened in the lives of ghosts from the past, then she could do so. She would never want to share her own history though, and indeed even if she did, who would believe it?

Her fingers were cramping now in the chill and she cupped her hands in front of her mouth and blew into the little fleshy hollow they made. The next moment was an epiphany of sorts. She heard the click of a radiator as it cooled against the wall, and with a moment of sudden brightness she realised that she could push the override button and turn on the heating with no reference to anyone else. She was totally in charge of her own existence. She laughed aloud into the night and then bit back the momentary mirth, it was unbecoming today of all days. Again, she stopped mid-thought. She turned and looked at the clock. It was just after three in the morning. The funeral was yesterday. It was in the past. Charlotte Mary was in the past.

Tears threatened, after so many years together it was as if a part of her own being had been left there in the crematorium, and yet... and yet. She was still here. She was alive. She was free – the final thought caused her to gulp. It had hovered just out of reach. Once they had known the terminal prognosis, it had implanted in her brain, but she had wrapped and rolled it in guilt and never acknowledged it until now.

She stood with her behind against the warming radiator and ran her hands back and forth along the ridged top, until it became too hot, and then she moved away.

She made tea and cut a thick slice of white bread for toast. She added a hunk of cheese to the plate and placed the snack on the dining table. This room, of all of them, felt empty and unwelcoming, the dark furniture glowering at her from corners. Sitting at her usual place, next to five empty chairs, was a lonely feeling. She put it all on a plastic tray from the kitchen and went back to her desk. She pushed aside her pens and notebook and then sat in her swivel chair. It felt silly to drape a napkin across her lap, but to eat without one, even now in this new world, was a step too far.

She had thought about this moment often during the last few weeks. She had held back from the final betrayal and now, when it was time, she was beset by doubt. She turned to the sideboard, hidden in a darker corner, and all that was visible of the portrait was a glint from the glass in the brown wooden frame. Nevertheless, she moved across the room and laid the picture face down.

She had few details to go on. She knew the aftermath. The final days were seared into her brain, a brand that she would carry with her to the grave. But of the beginnings, she had little really to work with.

She closed her eyes and played it over in her head. The first day: frantic arguments, pleading, desperate fear. There was the joy as well, and she wouldn't deny it, there was the wonder of it, but even through the awe, she had known it was wicked. It was as wrong as anything could be and now, all too late to be sure, she would see what she could do to make some sort of recompense for Charlotte Mary's great sin. Yes, and her own part in it, which was surely just as bad.

She knew the date and probable location from the timings that she had already worked out.

She took a sip of her tea, flexed her fingers, and began.

For a while, she looked at hospital sites and the records of births and deaths for Hampshire but without paying she couldn't get very far, and she couldn't pay until she knew just where to look. She had thought that she was adept at all this but was now overcome with the enormity of it, and her own inadequacy. She felt a moment of doubt and pushed it away. She was tired, that was all. She would look again tomorrow.

Chapter 3

Charlotte Mary had always been the driver. Lily had never learned, and the car that they had bought only two years ago would have to be sold. It might have been fun to learn but at this stage she must be realistic; though her mind was clear, her body might well let her down. She had been coping after all for the last months. She needed to organise transport for tomorrow to take her to see Mr Barnstaple, the solicitor.

The will.

She didn't want to do it but it was unavoidable. They had money in a joint account for general housekeeping, quite apart from her own funds. The house had always been in both their names, if there was anything else then it wasn't important. She had more than enough to live on, and savings which would pay for extras.

Nevertheless, it had to be faced, there may be things she would need to do. Charlotte Mary had outlived her brother and parents. There were hardly any relatives and the few friends that they had would surely not be mentioned. No, it would be a formality. If there were bills and costs, then the life insurance would cover that. Ah well, better to get it done now.

She was overcome by weariness. Her head was swimming with lack of sleep and she caught herself sitting motionless for minutes at a time, fingers frozen on the keys, her mind elsewhere.

Snippets and snaps of memory buzzed in and out of her thoughts: the day they had met, the first day of the upper sixth year. Charlotte Mary, a new girl at this most unlikely time in her school career. Brash and confident, and stunningly beautiful. Her long hair a great dark wave across slender shoulders and down her back, all the way to her tiny waist. Her brown eyes filled with laughter as they all turned to watch her swing across the quad, suitcase in hand, a bright canvas bag slung over her shoulder.

Lily had been smitten from that moment and when the new goddess had deigned to allow at first a friendship, and then so much more, she had convinced herself that her life was complete. At last she didn't need to hide who she was, what she felt, because, wonder of wonders, the new queen of the upper sixth was a sister in the flesh.

Her parents had been shocked when, at what seemed like the last minute, she had changed her university choices. But they went along with the changed plans, and helped with rent for the small flat the girls wanted to share. If they had misgivings about the relationship they kept it to themselves, and until they died never referred to Charlotte Mary as anything other than 'Lily's best friend'.

Yes, all had seemed golden, had been golden for a while. They had shocked some of their contemporaries, but they didn't care. They had hidden what needed to be hidden, when it was unavoidable – dangerous even – but then, as Charlotte Mary had always insisted, they should have what they wanted, do what they wanted, and it was no-one's business but their own.

She had been so brave and unconcerned about the approval of others, and Lily had grabbed onto her wonderful coat-tails and enjoyed the ride. How thrilling it had been, until in the end it became an obsession and very nearly their downfall.

It was later that their relationship had turned to – well, to what? To something else. Lily knew she had allowed herself to become secondary. It had begun just a couple of years after they graduated when Charlotte Mary had an affair with a woman from the publishing firm they both worked for. Lily thought her heart was truly broken. She hated the way she slid into the lesser role. At times desperate to escape what her life was becoming, but unable to face even one day without her partner. And yet, here it was. She was alone at last, and despite the memories and the quiver of unease at being fully in control of her own life for the first time since sixth form, she felt relieved. Relieved and released. Something stirred deep inside, a re-awakening of the person she once was.

She would be able to do this thing that she had craved for years. Her time working in the publishing industry would stand her in good stead, and with the miracle of the internet putting the whole world here in this Victorian terrace in Southsea, then she would succeed.

She climbed upstairs and paused at the door to the big double room at the front of the house. When the illness had become so advanced that sleeping together was impossible, she had moved out and into the back. Now there was no longer any need, it was time to move back.

Chapter 4

"Ms Bowers. Please come in. I hope everything went well yesterday. As well as these things can, at any rate." The solicitor was younger than Lily and it seemed wrong. For this she wanted an old man, one with thin, grey hair and cigar ash on his collar. But he was gone, along with so many others. Mr Turnbull had dealt with their affairs for a long time. He had always known exactly what their relationship was and they had felt his unexpressed disapproval. He would have preferred to pass them to one of the other partners. But he had acted for Lily's parents for years. He put money and business before any personal thoughts about their chosen way of life, held his tongue and stuck to polite but cool interaction with them. Charlotte Mary derived a cynical satisfaction from his situation and they had laughed at his discomfort, and tormented him with their presence.

Now Phillip Barnstable seemed perfectly at ease with her. Times had certainly changed and of course it was good, it was wonderful. But just today Lily longed for the odd, scary thrill of living outside the mainstream the way it had been. She knew they'd been lucky. Because of their choice of careers and ultimately the people they mixed with, they hadn't been harangued to any great degree and never felt in physical danger, and now, well now it was different.

"I am correct, aren't I, you never married or arranged a civil partnership?"

Lily smiled and shook her head. "There didn't seem much point. We had been together a long time. Since school." She stopped, suddenly too tired to do this now, to be forced to talk about the things that had gone. She had more important things to do. She wanted to be home in the warm house with a cup of coffee – the slow tick of the long case clock the only sound. This office, with the telephones and the computers, doors opening and closing, and the people, it was all too much. She sighed.

He moved on quickly. She imagined he would be challenged if she began to cry, but of course she wouldn't do that.

"So, I have had a look at things," He lifted one of the file boxes a couple of inches and then replaced it on the desk. There were two, one with her name and the other for Charlotte Mary. "I think you've handled things well. The house is now entirely yours, of course, once the formalities are completed, but I think my predecessor helped you to secure that?"

Lily inclined her head just once.

The excitement of buying their own place had been wonderful, and she remembered their laughter as they slammed the front door behind them on the first day. There had been no furniture, but they had brought Champagne and glasses. Lily had run out to the car to bring in the travel rug and the cushion from the back seat. They had made love on the floor of the big front bedroom. Afterwards, wrapped in the plaid blanket, they watched the light change as day gave way to evening. It was a precious memory that filled her eyes with moisture, and she needed a cough before she could speak again.

She straightened her shoulders. "Yes, we kept most things separate, we had our own bank accounts and so on. It was easier. Safer really."

He pursed his lips. It looked quite silly on his young face but she could see that over the years the small lines around his mouth would set as he became grey and dusty.

"Quite." He pulled out the envelope and extracted the pages of small type. "Mostly, I think this is just the way you would imagine. Of course, I will let you have your copy of this before you leave the office. She remembers a secretary with a small gift – I can deal with that if you wish?"

Lily nodded wordlessly again. She hadn't needed to come, had she? He could have sent the darned copy to her house and they could have spoken on the phone. She lifted her handbag from the chair beside her, held it on her lap as she slid forward on her seat. He took the hint.

"Right, well we must move on, mustn't we. You inherit what else there is. That will need to go to probate of course, but it's a formality. There is the small matter of – ahem – disposal. She has asked that her ashes be spread in the cellar of your home." He leaned forward. "I don't know how you feel about that, whether you had discussed it. If you are not comfortable with that request there is no legal reason for you to comply. It is entirely up to yourself. It's a little strange but perhaps it makes sense to you. I think that about covers things. There is a small box containing private papers also, not a bequest as such. She lodged it with us until such time as she died, but it is recorded as a joint asset. Do you want to take that with you or would you prefer me to send it by courier? It's not very big."

It was an old-fashioned box with a tiny hasp and staple fastening which had been secured with a piece of cord sealed with wax.

"I'll take it with me now. I'm using a taxi." Her hand, as she reached out, shook a little, and it was a struggle to keep her voice even as she gathered her things and stood in front of the desk. "Well, thank you for dealing with all of this. I'm sure it's all fine. Could you just send the copy of her will to me, in the post?" She held out her hand. Her fingers trembled and she had so wanted it to be strong and steady. She turned and pulled open the heavy wooden door before he had a chance to dash across and usher her through. Without a glance left or right, she stalked through the reception area, and out into a grey, chilly day.

There was no reason to believe that this would be anything important. Just a collection of old papers, photographs maybe. But why all the secrecy? Why hide them away? Could it be that Charlotte Mary had guessed what Lily would want to do? Had she, out of guilt or altruism, left the information? *Oh, please let it be so.* She turned away from the big, pale building and headed towards the railway station on The Hard, and a taxi.

Chapter 5

There was too much to do. She had brought the box into the house and placed it centrally on her desk. Of course, she could have snipped the little cord immediately, but she hoped that once opened it would fill her life. If the box had in it the information she wanted, then she needed to be ready to deal with whatever came next. Of course, it could all be wishful thinking but she had to clear the way so that there was no distraction. It had amused her friends, her family, this need to prepare and they had said it was Obsessive Compulsive Disorder, but it wasn't. It was just the way she was.

The wardrobes needed to be sorted first. Charlotte Mary had been taller, slimmer, always much more glamourous, and none of the expensive clothes would fit Lily's spreading frame. So, the charity shops could have the lot, hats, bags, scarves. There was nowhere she would be going to dress up, no longer any need to be smart. She pushed it all into cardboard boxes and stacked them in the sun room.

Once the cupboards and drawers were empty she brought her own things through. Twice she was overwhelmed with loss. It was true that her life hadn't been what she had hoped. The last years had been a sort of a pantomime of happiness played out before an audience of old friends. There were times when she had come to hate the sound of Charlotte Mary's strident voice, her bossy ways, her demands. There was, however, enough left of the old love, or at least the memory of it, to blow great gusts of grief across her soul.

It took most of the day to reclaim the master bedroom. Mrs Fleming would come on Wednesday to clean, but anyway, Lily polished and hoovered the room, re-establishing ownership. Then her way was clear to begin the bigger task.

It was late. She closed the curtains and made a cup of hot milk.

She closed her eyes and went back in her mind to the sunny, bright morning when the nightmare began.

* * *

Lily had walked along the seafront. She paused as always in front of the war memorial, read the names and then gazed out over the water towards the forts, grey and unlikely in the sparkly water of the Solent. She had marched briskly through the rose garden, and then through a growing throng of trippers and holiday-makers. No point in living on the coast and not taking full advantage, she had said. But lately Charlotte Mary hadn't wanted to join her, and if she was honest, Lily preferred the time alone, just an hour for peace and healing.

When she turned the corner into their own street she noted the little car wasn't parked at the kerb. Charlotte Mary hadn't said anything about going out, but she had been in a strange mood for a couple of weeks now. Secretive and withdrawn.

A quiver of unease turned Lily's stomach. After the previous year, after that horrible time when she had discovered the great betrayal of the affair, she had lived with a low-grade dread. There had been tears and tantrums, things said and things thrown, and there had been regret and in the end the coming together. Forgiveness and promises and yet still, she hadn't thought she would ever really be able to truly trust again.

Of course, she could have left, struck out on her own, divided what there was of their material life and gone away. But she hadn't. Cowardly and desperate, she had stayed and believed that surely one day she would find a way to be happy again. But it hadn't happened yet. Now with the car missing and the memories of phone calls cut short when she walked into the hallway, of papers stuffed hurriedly into the old brown briefcase, she remembered the feeling of insecurity and panicked.

The house was silent, the old clock that had cost a fortune and they both loved, measured the quiet passing of the day. The tap in the kitchen dripped into the sink. Automatically Lily turned it on and then off again, Charlotte Mary had still not managed to master the knack of dealing with its odd little idiosyncrasy. They had been intending to get a plumber to look at it and it hadn't happened. Not until the kitchen was upgraded years later. She walked into the dining room. In the middle of the dark oak dining table was a note.

Had to go out. Will be back this afternoon with a wonderful surprise.
X

Lily conjured in her mind what she had done next. Partly reassured, she had turned back into the kitchen, laid a hand on the kettle and felt the warmth. There was a mug on the draining board sitting in a tiny pool of water. So, she hadn't been gone long.

What time was it when she came back? How could she remember that? With so much emotion, so much fear and panic, how could she ever remember?

It had been a few hours, long enough for Lily to do the chores, prepare for the coming week and put together food for the evening.

She heard the car, the slam of its door, but hadn't gone to greet her partner. She was sulking. A day on her own lost in emptiness, and work in the morning with only a dull weekend with a bit of cleaning to look back on.

She had waited and wondered why it was taking so long, and eventually walked to the window and lifted the net curtains. She had seen the gate swinging closed and heard Charlotte Mary's key in the lock.

She had gone through to the hall as the door opened and their lives changed forever. The past becoming a different world in the blink of an eye.

Chapter 6

At first, it had looked just like bulky shopping. As she pushed into the hallway, closing the door with her behind, Charlotte Mary's arms had been full. A bulging bag dangled from one hand, and in the other she held a bundle of what, at a glance, appeared to be towels. She had dropped the bag to the floor and turned to where Lily stood, at the entrance to the lounge.

Her eyes were brimming with excitement, her generous mouth smiling broadly. She held the bundle in both arms, lowered her face to it for a moment, and then with a sort of flourish held it out before her.

For an instant Lily had thought a puppy, a kitten perhaps, and her heart had sunk. More work, more cleaning up to do. But Charlotte Mary's beam of pure joy made the mundane reaction seem unworthy. She forced her face into an enquiring look, tipping her head to one side. Moving across the carpet she murmured, already adjusting her voice to the presence of a small animal, "Now, then. What's this? What have we got here?" And then she had been close enough to see, and she had cried out in shock, her hands flying to cover her mouth. "What the hell, Charlotte?"

The baby was sleeping. It moved a little at the sudden noise and Charlotte Mary began to rock, gentle but awkward, the movement unfamiliar to her. "Shh, shh. He's asleep."

By now Lily was standing close enough to touch the tiny fingers, to stroke the soft little cheek. She smiled down at him. "Oh, Charlotte. Whose is this? Why have you got him? I wish you'd said, I would have made sure the house was warmer. Why didn't you take me with you? What a little treasure. How long is he staying? Whose is he?"

* * *

Sitting in the living room, the colour beginning to leach from the day, she could hear the tick of the clock. It was as if she was back there, in that moment, still waiting for the answers to her questions. Still waiting for her life to be turned on its head, never to be righted again.

She shuddered and swallowed down a sob. In many ways, it had already been too late, but if she had been stronger, more secure, and if the instant of absolute love for the tiny boy hadn't taken her quite so much by surprise, that would have been the moment to save them. To save them all.

* * *

"He's ours. I got him for us."

"What? What on earth do you mean? Don't be so silly. Who is he? Where did he come from?"

"I don't know who he is. Not yet. I thought maybe Peter, but we'll have to decide. There's time though, we ought to register him but that's a bit complicated for the moment – soon though, and I thought we could hyphenate. What do you think of Peter Stone-Bowers? I think that flows better than Bowers-Stone, though that does have a lovely feel to it as well. But we must talk about it. Let's get organised. He'll be waking up soon, and he'll need a bottle."

In the maelstrom of disbelief, Lily was aware of Charlotte Mary pointing with her foot towards the bag on the floor. "All the stuff is in there. I don't think I forgot anything, but we have to sterilize the bottles. I think it takes a set amount of time. There are some nappies and things as well."

"No, no, wait. Just stop for a minute. What are you talking about? What do you mean he's ours? You're not making sense."

The child moved again and made a small noise.

"Hush now, Lily, you'll frighten him. Look, take him. I'll do the other stuff, the bottle and what have you. I've been told how. Go on, take him. Go through to the living room and cuddle him for a while. You're going to love him. Isn't he perfect? Here." She held him out, a gift, an offering. "Go on, take him while I sort us out."

Lily recalled backing away, shaking her head, trying to organise her thoughts. "Where did he come from, Charlotte? Who does he belong to?"

"I've told you, he's ours. I arranged it all."

"Oh God, you didn't steal him? Tell me you haven't taken him!"

"Of course I haven't." There had been a flash of anger, gentled by the need to keep the noise to a minimum, to keep the atmosphere calm for the baby. "What do you take me for? I'm not going to tell you. I am sworn to secrecy. You must see that. But I wanted something for us. To bring us back together and it's going to be such fun. Don't worry, I've sorted everything out."

"How do you mean, what have you sorted out? I can't take this in. What on earth have you done?"

She had followed into the living room and watched as Charlotte Mary had made a sort of nest on the settee, lining up the cushions along the edge, and then laying the little boy in the space in the middle. She adjusted the blankets and stroked his cheek.

"Now then, I realise it's a surprise, but I knew you'd try to stop me and there's no need. This is going to be so good for us, don't you see? It makes us into a proper family. I know there'll be complications, I know we're going to have to get our stories straight and what have you, but we can do that. We can do anything, you know that, with me you can do anything. Whatever we want, we can have. Look how we are here. Look how we have this house, this life. There's no reason for us not to have this as well. I've been thinking about it forever, since last year, that nastiness, my mistake. It's so obvious. We are a proper family now, Charlotte, Lily and Peter."

"No, no, this is madness, you've lost your mind. What are you thinking?"

But it had been to no avail and the smell of him, the sight of him so vulnerable amongst the cushions, his tiny fist curled against his cheek had melted her heart. The next words had sealed their fate. "She didn't want him, you see. His mummy didn't want him, so I have brought him home. I had to wait a while and it's been so hard keeping it a secret, but now he's here and he's ours." She had wrapped her arms around Lily and rocked with her just as she had in the hallway cradling the baby. "Oh, Lily, I do love you and this is going to be perfect. Just trust me and it'll be perfect."

* * *

Lily sighed. From the distance of years, it was all so obvious what she should have done. She should have been stronger, should have insisted on knowing all the ins and outs of the terrible business. But she hadn't, she had leaned into the warm, strange, baby scent that lingered on Charlotte Mary's clothes and closed her eyes and given in, yet again.

Chapter 7

Lily had always been able to remember the first time she held him. The strange weight, not heavy but not as light as the kitchen scales told them he was. She hadn't been afraid, not the way she heard other people were afraid. She never thought she would hurt him, never worried that she might drop him, for she knew from the first moments that she would protect him with her life. Would have done, if it had been asked of her. But it wasn't. That wasn't to be the sacrifice.

Charlotte Mary had made his feed and insisted that Lily give the bottle to him. She knew of course that holding Peter, and giving him food, was the way to make her bond with him, and it worked.

As the boy had taken the milk, Charlotte Mary made them tea and then sat on the settee, and reached now and again, touched his feet, his fingers, his face. "I have ordered some things, from Knight and Lee. They won't come until tomorrow. Just a cot for him, some bedding and more nappies. I am amazed at how much you have to have. Later we'll need a pram to take him for walks. Then a highchair and, oh, all manner of things. Tonight, we can make a bed in the big laundry basket." They had grinned at the idea, and the big wicker basket had been perfect, lined with blankets and resting on the dresser.

"How do you know? How did you find out what we need?"

"I borrowed some books from the library. I've been planning and scheming for such a long time. From when I knew that we could have him. I have thought it all through. We can ring the office tomorrow. I'll do it, I'll tell them that we both have nasty colds and we will be taking the week off. That will give us a chance to organise things and I have already found the name of a woman who does baby and childcare. I made a call, told her I was asking on behalf of my sister. I used your name."

They had done this before, when they felt it was better to keep their true relationship private. Sisters sharing a home, it was a common thing. Less so as the war years drew away but still nothing untoward. No-one had ever questioned it, and Lily simply nodded.

"But how can this work? How can this be alright?"

"Well of course it can. We are financially sound. We have our own home. We are intelligent, mature women. For heaven's sake, anyone can have a baby, even girls straight from school can have a baby. But we have so much more to offer him. Think of all the women who, after the war, brought up children who had been born to other people. Sisters, daughters, grannies, just neighbours. He needed someone like us, it's all fine."

Lily had thought often that it had been a clue. The reference to a girl straight from school. She had used that to try and convince herself that they were doing a good thing. She built a picture of a young woman, frightened and in trouble. A desperate child who they were rescuing from the mess his careless mother had created. In the event, it had been such a very short and precious time that none of it had ever really mattered. The baby carer, the pram, the high chair. None of it had been needed. The cot had been used just briefly and then afterwards they had burned it in the back garden, sobbing in the smoky air and clinging to each other in despair.

When he was first sick, Charlotte Mary had insisted it was normal. "His little stomach is only just getting used to food. All babies are sick, it's in the books. It's nothing."

But it hadn't been nothing. It had come so very quickly that by the time they realised, it was too late and he drifted away, his mewling cries less and less until they just watched him leave them.

They had been guilty, of course they had, but it had been such a frightening time and she wasn't clear just what they were guilty of – legally. They should have called the doctor, but he would have wanted to know where the mother was. They considered, briefly, just leaving him at the hospital, but he had wrapped his baby fingers so tightly around their hearts that they couldn't do it. They tried dripping teaspoons of sugar water into the tiny mouth. They cleaned him and rocked him and by the time they understood how very ill he was, it was over.

The grief did something dreadful to Charlotte Mary. The disappointment, the sense of loss – all of it turned her hard. Where Lily sobbed, and staggered down into the cellar to hide in the dark and murmur words of regret and sorrow, Charlotte Mary took herself off to parties, to weekends in London with the young people who they worked with. She wouldn't speak of him, wouldn't consider telling anyone. "Don't be ridiculous, it would ruin us. Can you imagine the fuss there would be? We would lose everything, and for what? He's gone Lily, let him go."

Locked together by the awful guilt, and the lying, and the unnamed crime, they were like tigers sharing a cage. They pushed and prodded at each other and niggled and nagged.

They hid it well – none of their friends, none of their work colleagues were aware of the disintegration of the idyll.

And so it had been until the fast living, the cigarettes and drink, and ultimately the drugs had taken their toll. Lily believed it was grief, swallowed down and held back, and the fury at the way it had all turned out. She believed that the darkness inside her partner had become a physical thing, and in the end, it had killed her.

Chapter 8

The morning was bright, birds flicked back and forth across the garden, and the sun through the window was warm. Dust motes danced and spiralled in the living room. Lily didn't feel the comfort of the sun, or hear the birdsong. It was outside of her world, experienced through a grey veil. With the morning had come the now familiar sense of doom and emptiness. She had this one great task to perform and then she was done.

She went into the cellar. The flowers were limp and drooping, and she put them aside to take to the compost bin. She had brought a new candle for the little glass holder. She kindled the tiny flame and sat for a while watching it burn, steady and bright in the stillness of the damp room. It might be a fire risk, but she didn't see how and couldn't bring herself to care. She left it glimmering in the darkness, climbed back to the kitchen, and gently closed the door.

That done, she was ready. She walked to the desk and pulled the small box towards her. She slit through the wax seal. Holding the lid with both hands she flipped it open.

There wasn't much. She had expected a letter. Declarations of love, regret, and perhaps an apology, and of course the vital information. She felt a sharp sting of disappointment that there was nothing like that. There was a small brown paper bag, the sort that vegetables used to come in. The top was folded over and it was tucked in, filling the small space. She pulled at one corner, gently. It looked fragile.

She peered into the bag. There were just a few items and they had slid into the bottom. She tipped it gently and everything inside slithered out into a little pile on the blotter.

There was a card, smaller than a postcard and flimsier, a short piece of blue plastic and a folded paper. Lily pulled the box towards her, peered inside, but there was nothing more.

She lifted the plastic strip and turned it over. Her breath caught in her throat as she handled the tiny bracelet. It had been cut just near to the plastic popper fastening. In a wider part, a piece of card had been slipped behind a clear window. The writing was faded but still legible, *Baby Robertson.*

The same name was written in a neat hand on the top of the blue card. There was a date, a weight and some sort of code. Just letters that meant nothing to her.

Baby Robertson.
24th July 1978.
7lb 6ozs.

Her body had forgotten how to breathe. It was only when the room tipped in dizziness that she realized she was no longer drawing air into her lungs. She gasped, and reached trembling fingers to the small piece of paper. It was a name and address. Charlotte Mary's writing, faint after many years, but unmistakable. A time, and the figure – five hundred pounds. There were two signatures, Charlotte Mary's, oh so familiar, and another. A 'C' she thought or possibly an 'L', followed by Robertson.

It was all there, so clear, so obvious. It was the answer to most of Lily's problems, the first step in the journey she had to make. But how very heart-breaking it was. Such hope, dashed. Such joy, defeated, and such a small, small price to pay for a life.

Charlotte Mary had not let him go unmarked into the beyond. She had simply waited until she herself had moved on, and then left it to Lily to tidy up the dreadful loose ends. She had known that was what would happen, and in either kindness or guilt, had pointed the way, handed on the baton.

Her dying had taken such a long time, and the sorry state of their relationship had precluded real grief but now, on this bright day, in the comfort of their home, Lily missed her friend, her lover. She lowered her head to the desk and let the tears flow. Sorrow for Charlotte Mary, and for the tiny life that had touched theirs so briefly but with the force of a tsunami, and had ultimately destroyed them.

Baby Robertson.

She opened the document on her computer and alongside the name Peter, she put in the new information. It felt wrong to add the name that they had chosen, the one that he had worn for such a short time, to the name that was rightfully his, but to call him *Baby* wasn't right either. So, there it was, his two worlds coming together, Peter Robertson.

He couldn't have a birth certificate in the other name. Charlotte Mary had said that they would need to register him, so all the plans were changed. She didn't need to do anything the way she had intended. It was going to be a different sort of search. She would find the address in Bath. She would go and find her, that other woman.

Surely, she had a right to know. She must have wondered over all these years just what had happened to her son. Now that Lily knew she was nearing the end of her life she must act, and make sure that his family knew just what had happened to him and yes, she must arrange for him to go home.

He may have siblings, aunts and uncles. No grandparents surely after all this time, but he may well have extended family and when she was gone there would be people who would carry his memory forward. He would not be forgotten.

Chapter 9

It was almost too easy. Instead of surfing the net, tracing records, fighting for information, she had it all at her fingertips. A piece of paper with an address and a surname. She typed the details into Google Earth, and watched as the image swooped into a square almost in the centre of the city. Not far at all from the railway station, walking distance for certain.

Of course, there were no guarantees. The chances that this person was still there after all this time had to be slim, but it was a beginning.

Even buying the train ticket was straightforward. No need to even leave the house, all done online. She would go on Monday. The weekend was a bad idea, it would be busy on Saturday, and Sunday, the trains may not be reliable. Monday, mid-morning, arriving in Bath at lunchtime.

Now that the thing was underway she was excited. She had often thought of Peter's mother. If she had been correct, and Charlotte Mary had inadvertently given things away by referring to a young girl, then she would have been sixteen maybe, seventeen, or even younger. So, now she would be late middle-aged – maybe a bit beyond that.

Very likely still working, with a family grown up, and even a grandchild. She paused, that could have been her. If it hadn't gone so tragically wrong, would she now have grandchildren? A family, people who cared and whom she could visit, whom she could love? It would have been a strange background for him, but things had come so far that today it wouldn't really matter that his home had two women and no man. She smiled — what would they have been called? — ah, it was no good, there were no grandchildren, so they had never been called anything. There was nothing but sadness and regret, and the memory of horror.

She didn't feel hungry exactly, but she had to have something when she took her medication. She warmed some soup and ate it standing in the kitchen. She was no longer pretending to set the dining table. They had always done it, napkins and water glasses, china and shining cutlery. What was the point? It was all play acting anyway. In the early days, they had embraced these little rituals. But as their partnership disintegrated they had become the glue that held their lives together, and now there was no longer any need. She hadn't yet been reduced to lounging on the sofa with her meal, so if she did eat at all, she did it on the run, a quick snack, undeserving of any performance.

Late in the night she went back down to the cellar. It had become familiar to her again as it had been all those years ago. No hesitation now on the creaky stairs. She replaced the candle and sat for just a little while.

At first, she hadn't spoken aloud but slowly she began to verbalise the things in her mind. She talked to him, as you would to a child. "I'm going to go on a train, Peter. It's not very far. I might find your mummy. Your real mummy. I'm going to tell her about you and what happened. I think she will be sad, but at least she'll know and then we can decide what to do next.

"Next week I'm bringing…" She paused. She had been going to say Aunty Charlotte. But they had never been that. She didn't know what they had been but surely, given time, they would have come up with something different: Mama one and two, or Mummy Charlotte, Mummy Lily perhaps. Anyway she left it. He couldn't hear her and he couldn't care that the ashes were coming back to the house. She hadn't decided yet what to do about all that. She didn't want to spread them down here on the damp earth. She couldn't walk on them and she couldn't contemplate spreading them on Peter's grave. Leaving them at the garden of rest was too much of a rebellion. She glanced around. Perhaps she would just leave them here in the container, or whatever they came in. Surely it wasn't an urn. That had become a bit comic, they must have something new. Maybe a little bag, or some sort of a box. The truth was that she really didn't want to bother at all. Charlotte Mary was gone, why couldn't she just be gone? She sighed and pushed herself up from her perch on the ledge. She was a stupid old woman sitting in the cellar talking to the ground.

Chapter 10

The train was about half full. Lily found a single seat in a corner. She wanted to be left alone. It would have been more comfortable to stretch out in a four-seat arrangement, but that would have meant there would be others. She would feel obliged to smile at them, to nod and acknowledge that, *here we all are together on a journey*, and she didn't want any of that. She wanted to sit with her shoulder leaning against the cold, hard interior of the train and to close her eyes and listen to the mumble and hum around her, and so she did.

The sleepless nights had made her mind foggy and, as the train roared on through Hampshire and into Somerset, she was assaulted by short daydreams. Memories that she didn't want and didn't need flickered in and out of her consciousness: the vision of herself and Charlotte Mary wrapping the tiny body in a blanket, tucking it into a transport box that had been kept because it was solid wood and too good to throw away.

The soil in the cellar had been hard packed, and the top layer tough to break. But once they were through the crust of it they had quickly made the hole big enough, deep enough. She remembered how they had baulked at stamping it down, walking on the new grave, so they had smoothed it over and over with the back of the spade and then patted it with their hands. Charlotte Mary had lost her mind for a moment and begun to thump with her fists, crying and wailing, an animal noise that played and replayed in Lily's ears for days. She had wrapped her arms around Charlotte Mary's shoulders and held her tight until the storm passed, and then wiped away the tears and the snot with the hem of her dirty cardigan. They hadn't wanted to leave him, and sat for hours in the dark, until eventually they crawled up into the house on hands and knees, feeling in the gloom for the wooden steps and sobbing and gulping with grief.

The next morning Lily had felt ill, battered and exhausted. Watching Charlotte Mary at the dresser, smoothing concealer over swollen eyes, and sweeping the red lipstick in a gash across her pale face, she had been surprised. "What are you doing?"

"I'm getting ready for the office. You need to get a move on. You'll be late."

"What on earth do you mean? We can't go into the office, what are you thinking?"

Charlotte Mary had swivelled towards her. "So, what should we do Lily? There is nothing to do, it's over."

"But we have to…"

And Charlotte Mary had simply nodded. They had made the decision already, dreadful mistake that it had been. They had hidden him away and pretended that he had never been.

That had been the first day of the torment, and if Lily had known, if she had seen what the rest of her days would hold, she would have clambered down into the cellar and joined him there in the dark and been with him for all this time. But she hadn't, she allowed herself to be persuaded that it was for the best, that they should move along, and all would be well.

She jerked awake now and looked around. The woman on the other side of the aisle glanced across and smiled. "Soporific, aren't they? Trains. Rocking you off to sleep."

Lily wanted to cry.

She took out the map printed from the Google Earth image and followed the crowd out of the station and into the town centre.

It had been years since she had been to Bath and the redevelopment left her completely unsure. But she didn't need to go into the shopping area. She turned and headed away from the hustle, across the Halfpenny Bridge and towards Widcombe.

It was a steep climb up Lyncombe Hill but only a few hundred yards to Southcote Place. She paused on the corner of the quiet square. There were birds in the trees and a black and white cat in the grass. Her shoe heels clumped loudly against the old stone flags. Her heart was pounding, her palms damp, and she wanted nothing more than to turn and run.

The houses were a mixed bag. Some looked grand and well maintained, blinds and swagged curtains at gleaming windows. Tidy gardens with tasteful ornaments. Others, including the one before her now, were obviously converted into flats. She took the few steps across the pavement, through the metal gate and up a short pathway.

She glanced down. This basement, so different from the one back in Southsea, had been made into accommodation. She could see a neat kitchen, with a table and chairs and a baby seat on the floor. She turned her face away and peered at the bell pushes beside the door. There were no names, no numbers. She reached a trembling finger towards the lowest of the round, brass buttons.

Chapter 11

Only the hum of traffic on the main road at the bottom of the hill disturbed the chilly afternoon. There was no answer to her first attempt so, after a couple of minutes, Lily tried the second bell. She heard the distant sound of feet on the stairs, the door swung open and a tall male figure appeared in the dim hallway.

"Oh, hi."

"Hello. I'm sorry to bother you but I'm trying to trace an old friend."

"Right." He was young, good-looking and dressed in jeans and a smart jacket with a blue T-shirt underneath. He carried a cycling helmet in his hand.

"It's a long time ago and they may well have moved by now, but this is the last address I have."

"Okay. So, who was it?"

"Robertson, her name was Robertson." Behind her back Lily had crossed her fingers. It was such a tenuous thread after all this time, and she wasn't sure what she would do if it unravelled at this stage.

He shook his head and pulled his mouth downwards in a negative gesture. She felt her heart sink.

"No, not here. I know the names of all the tenants. There's no Robertson." He stepped forward now and grabbed the door handle, Lily moved backwards. What more was there to say, after all.

"Oh, hang on. Robertson?"

"Yes, that's it."

"Ah right, it's the owners, isn't it?"

"Is it?"

"Yeah, I'm pretty sure that's the name. I rent, through an agency of course, but I'm sure that's the name on the lease."

"Oh, how wonderful."

"Yeah. You should call Burk and Brownlees. They're based in Bristol. Have you got your phone, a piece of paper?"

She took out her mobile and inserted the name and the number into her contacts list. "That's so kind of you. Thank you so much. You've been very kind."

"No problem. Sorry, I really will have to go now. Good luck."

"Thank you. Thank you so much."

So, not a failure at all. As she turned from the door Lily felt elated, there was the real chance that this was going to work out smoothly.

She walked into the town centre and found a little café. It was the first time she had been in this sort of place since Charlotte Mary had become too ill to eat out. Nobody looked her way, everyone was busy living. So, this was what was in store. For whatever time was remaining she would be invisible, of no interest to anyone. It should have made her sad, even more depressed, but today at least, she didn't mind at all. She didn't want to talk to people she didn't know, she didn't really want to talk to people she did know, not any more. All she wanted was to finish what she had to do, and then to be left alone in the quiet of her fading days.

She wasn't going to waste time so she took out her phone. She knew it was unlikely the rental agency would simply give out contact details, but it was worth a try, and it had to start somewhere. She couldn't face traveling through to Bristol, finding the offices only to be told they couldn't help her, and then all the way back to Bath Spa to wait for another train. She was tired, but there was a half an hour to kill, so she sat in the window of the coffee shop, ordered more tea, and dialled the number.

"Burk and Brownlees, Emma speaking. How may I help you?"

"I am calling to ask about one of your landlords." There was nothing to be gained by obfuscation so she stated her case baldly. Either this would work or it wouldn't. It was a first step, that was all.

"Are you a tenant?"

"No, I am trying to trace an old friend and I believe you act for her." She'd never been comfortable with lying but this whole situation was built on deception so, though this lie upon lie distressed her, the truth wouldn't serve.

"I'm afraid I can't help you with that. I can't give out contact details of our clients."

"Ah, I thought that might be the case. Well, thank you." She was about to hang up and a second thought stilled her finger, where it hovered over the button. What was there to lose after all?

"I wonder if you could do me a favour then?"

"A favour?"

"Yes, my friend is the landlord, or rather the owner, of some flats in Bath. Do you think you could pass my number on?"

"I think that would be okay. But we have quite a number of properties in Bath, do you know the address?"

"Yes, yes of course." She heard the clatter of a keyboard as she recited the address.

"Okay, I know who that is. Do you want to give me your name and details?"

"Yes, thank you. It's…" she paused. "It's Charlotte Mary Stone." She had to swallow hard before she could continue and recite the telephone number. After the call, she slid the phone into her bag and picked up her cup of tea. Her hands shook and she needed to replace her drink on the saucer for a minute. She closed her eyes and drew in a couple of steadying breaths.

If there were no calls in the next couple of days, then what? Plans began to form, crazy plans, illogical. She could rent a flat in Bath, and that way would secure the owner's address. No, that was ridiculous, she couldn't find out the name of a landlord as a precursor to renting a place. She would just have to hope for the best and if this didn't work then she would find another way.

Lily's mind calmed a bit as she strolled back through the town centre to the station. She sat on the draughty platform, looking across the tracks in the direction of Lansdowne Hill.

What had it been like? Had Peter's mother lived there, hiding her pregnancy until it was impossible to do so? Had she brought him home from the hospital to that house years before, or had she simply left him somewhere, and made the journey with empty arms and a broken heart? Maybe it would be possible to ask these questions, gently and kindly. She could fill in some of the old blanks and it might help. For the moment, all there was to do was to wait and hope that the phone would ring.

* * *

She walked through her front door into the warm house with a sigh of relief. She was exhausted.

The living room was in darkness except for a faint ambient glow. She didn't close the curtains but sat in the gloom, and let the weariness have its way. She shut her eyes and drifted back to the golden past. Their joyous graduation, the dancing, the drinking, the friends who had all disappeared. Why was that? Had they in some way given off an air of tragedy in spite of efforts, mainly by

Charlotte Mary, to present a happy face to the world? Had the deteriorating relationship made them poor company, though they had been better in a crowd?

Ah well, it didn't matter much anymore.

She spiralled into the comfort of sleep and dreamed of small boys and little hands folded in her own. Of holidays by the sea, of first days at school and of a young man leaning down to kiss her brow. Cold tears leaked from under her sleeping lids and dried on her wrinkled cheek.

Chapter 12

She carried the phone with her everywhere. Even when she took a shower she placed it on the top of the toilet cistern, propped so that she would see if the screen lit up. She left the curtain open, and then had to mop soapy water from the floor.

She was distracted and edgy all day with little to do and tried to fill the time with odd jobs, and distract her mind with the plans that it was possible to make.

She called into a charity shop in Palmerston Road, and asked them to arrange to send someone with a car. The boxes of Charlotte Mary's leftovers were bulky, and she knew she couldn't carry them through the streets.

Lily wondered if she would like to work in one of these places, to fill her remaining time with 'good works'. Maybe mixing with other people would unpeel the layers of despair that were growing heavier with each day. She knew she wouldn't do it though, there was only room for the Peter situation, and she shrugged the musings aside.

A young woman called in the afternoon and helped to carry the stuff from where Lily had piled it by the front door. They stuffed it into the boot and rear seat of her car.

She stood on the path and watched until the car turned at the end of the road, the little indicator flashing brightly against the grey day. Then she went back into the house which was now, for the first time, devoid of Charlotte Mary. Empty except for her great sin buried in the basement, and part of the fabric of the building.

When the phone rang, she dragged it from her pocket, her heart pounding with excitement, until she read the number of the Funeral Directors.

"Hello, this is Muriel. How are you, Lily? How are you getting along?" She was sickly sweet, this woman, and Lily wanted her to go away.

"I'm fine, thank you. Yes, just fine." She knew she sounded cold, but felt wrung out, empty inside, and had no reserves to draw on except automatic response.

"Good. Well that's good, that's the spirit. You just have to move along, don't you? I am calling because I have had confirmation that you can collect the ashes, whenever it's convenient. The times are given in the information booklet. We did give you the booklet, didn't we?"

"Yes, I have it. Thank you."

"Well, that's about it I think. Did you purchase an urn?"

"No, I don't think so, I didn't know that was my responsibility."

"Oh dear, that was in the booklet."

"I didn't see that, I didn't read the thing."

"You could call them, but if not they will provide a temporary container. You shouldn't worry, it will be taken care of. Don't get upset about it."

Lily felt a stirring of anger, she hated to be spoken to as if she was simple-minded, and as she aged it seemed that it happened more and more often. She couldn't bear to be treated as though she had no experience of life, that there was nothing to her except the decrepit old thing that she had become. "I wasn't worried to be honest, I didn't think that I would be expected to walk through the streets with the ashes loose in my hand. Although these days who knows?"

There was a short silence and then Muriel gathered herself and spoke again, quieter this time and a little less simpering, "Lily, I do hope you were happy with our services. If you have time there is a place on the website for client feedback and we would be very grateful. Of course, if there was anything that didn't quite reach the standard you expected, we would prefer you to discuss that with us, rather than make negative comments. Were you happy?"

This was outrageous. Lily tried to adjust to changing attitudes but this was too much. She floundered for a response, and in the end simply said, "thank you," and disconnected the call. She threw the phone onto the table and then as her outburst replayed in her mind she began to laugh. It was a little hysterical to be sure but it was laughter nonetheless. Oh, Charlotte Mary would have been proud of that.

She lay in the front bedroom, amongst the familiar shadows and the strange emptiness until it became unbearable, and then slid from the big bed, pulling the duvet with her. She went down to the living room. There she curled against the arm of the settee, drooping and drifting in half sleep until the birds began to chatter in the garden hedge. The pair of great crows that came every morning to a roof opposite drove her from the room with their screeching.

She was stirring sugar into her second mug of coffee when the ringing called her back, dashing in her bare feet across the hall carpet to snatch up the vibrating mobile from the coffee table.

It was an unknown number and she steadied herself against the wall as she answered. "Hello, Lily Bowers."

The voice was deeper than she was expecting, rough and obviously male. "I want to speak to... Charlotte Mary Stone. I was given this number."

In her excitement, she had forgotten the name that she had left with the agents. She panicked, what was she to do?

"Oh, yes, yes, this is Charlotte's phone, can I help you?"

"I don't know. I just had a message to call this number. I don't have a clue what it's about. Can I talk to her?"

"She's not here just now. Who am I speaking to please? Could I take a message?"

"Well, as I say I haven't a clue what this is about, something about an old friend. I don't have any friends, old or new for that matter, called Charlotte. I haven't got a lot of time to waste on stuff like this. If it's some sort of sales scam then, well, sod off really."

"No, no, wait. It isn't a scam, I'm sure it's not. She wouldn't – well we wouldn't do that. Who am I speaking to please?"

"Terry Robertson. Look, if it's about a flat then you have to go through the agent, I don't deal direct with tenants, that's why I pay all that money in fees."

"No, it's not that. I don't need a flat. Look, if you are Mr Robertson, well I don't mean if, I'm sure you are. Oh sorry, you've caught me unprepared. Look, I do know what this is about. Charlotte Mary was trying to trace an old friend. She had an address in Bath and it turns out that you are the owner. I'm sorry there must have been some mistake." As she said it disappointment flooded through her and she sank to the chair, deflated. "It was a woman that we were trying to find, C. Robertson."

"Well, there are no women, not any more. There was my granny and my mum but they've gone now, both of them."

"Oh."

He didn't question that she didn't know the name, only the initial, but in a more thoughtful tone he continued, "Well, maybe it was my mum. Look, not wishing to be rude, but how old is this Charlotte? My mum would have been fifty-eight, but she died a couple of years ago. Is that who your friend was looking for? Carol, her name was."

Yes, Lily's heart jumped with the thrill. "I am so sorry to hear that she died. I wonder though, would you mind if Charlotte gave you a call?"

"Well, I don't see the point to be honest. Mum's gone and I don't know your friend."

"No, I realise that, but there is something Charlotte specifically wanted to talk about, something from the past and well, I think it might be of interest to you."

"Oh, if it's to do with reunions, family history all that sort of stuff I'm not interested thanks. No, I don't think there's any need."

She had to stop him, he was about to ring off. "No, it's not that. It's to do with erm… it's to do with a legacy."

"How do you mean?"

"Something that Charlotte was given by your mum, to keep. Well I am almost sure it was your mum. That was the address we had, the one in Bath. Did she live in the house in Southcote Place?" She could tell by the change in his tone that she had his interest.

"Yes, that was where they all lived, until we had it converted. So, when can I call her? Or maybe she could give me a bell."

"Could she meet you?"

"Yes, I suppose that would work. Are you in Bath?"

"No, we're not, but she'd be more than happy to travel to Bath, if that's convenient."

"Alright then, I have to say I'm quite tickled by the idea of having something of my mum's. What about tomorrow? I have to go through anyway."

"Yes, excellent. That would be fine. Where would you like to meet? About lunchtime perhaps, would that be convenient? Maybe somewhere you could have coffee?"

"Tell you what, how about twelve o'clock in the Crystal Palace. Do you know it?"

"No, not really."

"Well it's easy to find. Down behind the cathedral in the square with that big old tree. Anyone will be able to tell you."

"Right, fine. We'll see you tomorrow, oh well no, not me I won't be able to come but Charlotte, I mean Charlotte."

"Great."

And he was gone. Lily slid to the floor and lowered her head to her knees. For a while thoughts jumbled against each other, but as they settled and straightened, she began to smile. She'd done it, she'd found her, maybe, just maybe. And then she reconsidered, she hadn't really. For after all this, she was dead.

Nevertheless, Charlotte Mary, with the little box and the old paper bag had seemingly led her to the baby's mother and his brother. The thought was strange and unsettling, perhaps a half-brother, but nevertheless a blood relative of their little dead boy. Someone with his DNA. It made him real again in a way that she hadn't expected. She went down to the basement to tell him, to whisper in the darkness about his mummy – his other mummy – and how sad it was that she would never know what had happened to him. "Maybe," she said, "maybe you are together, perhaps it works that way and you found her after all." She lit the new candle she had brought and then climbed back upstairs to find things to occupy her, and to organise the trip in the morning.

Chapter 13

Lily was very early. It was a bright day, a little cold but sunny. She walked by the river and watched ducks sliding down the weir; strolled up to the cathedral and past it, across the paved square, and she headed towards the great old tree.

The pub was busy, but there was a small table beside the fireplace. She could see the door, and watch the passing crowd through the window. Always, when she had thought of Peter, grown and maturing, not dead in the box in the cellar, she had given him strong limbs, a bright smile, and dark, curly hair. She had imagined that, naturally, he would be taller than her, taller even than Charlotte Mary's five feet eight inches, and of course, he was handsome. She had drawn this picture from desire in the absence of fact. The tiny child that she had held for such a short time had carried the blueprint, but that was all. The Peter of her daydreams was no more than imagination and wish.

The door opened and a thin young man came through, his mousy hair blown by the wind. She turned her eyes back towards the window. He was due anytime now. The door opened again, but this time a young couple scuttled in, giggling and pushing at each other. She snorted a little with impatience, turned back to stare at the manufactured flames in the hearth.

"Charlotte Mary. Is that you?" His voice was recognisable, the one that she had spoken to on the phone. When she turned though, and looked into the pale blue eyes, she was swept, not by thrill and excitement, but by a wave of intense disappointment.

This was not Peter's brother. This was not a tall good-looking young man filling her eyes with the reality of her imagination. She had overlooked him. She had seen him enter and dismissed him, and now here he was, raising his eyebrows in query, and laying a thin, boyish hand on the back of the chair. "I reckoned it must be, you being on your own and…" He had been about to refer to her age, hadn't he? She saw a slight flush of embarrassment as he caught himself and bit back the words.

She half stood, changed her mind and flopped back onto the seat. He hadn't held out a hand to her, so she placed hers on the table, flat at each side of the cup and saucer. "Yes, Charlotte," she nodded, "and you must be Mr Robertson, Terry was it?" She knew that she sounded unfriendly but had taken an unreasonable and instant dislike to him, because of his failure to be what she wanted him to be. His poor manners had compounded the problem and she felt despair and disappointment immerse the hope and excitement.

He pointed to her cup. "Do you want another one? Coffee or tea, is it?"

"No, thank you." The old Lily poked her head above the recently built wall of self-preservation. "I'd like a glass of wine please. Red, something heavy."

"Oh, erm… Okay, right you are, coming up."

She didn't watch him walk away, instead her eyes closed and she breathed deeply. It wasn't his fault, none of it, and she mustn't antagonise him. He may know the story of how his little, lost brother came to be. It would make her rapid journey to the end of life so much better if she had the whole picture. It wouldn't change what happened, but it would be a fine thing after all this time.

"I hope this is alright. A Bordeaux."

She nodded and smiled at him as Terry Robertson dragged a chair across the floor, and then with his pint of lager already half-drunk in one great gulping swallow, he looked her straight in the eyes.

"So, your friend, the one on the phone. She said you had something of my mum's. I can't imagine what it could be. So, what's all this about?"

"Tell me about her."

"How do you mean? I thought you knew her."

She had known it was going to be difficult, pretending and lying and straight away she had failed. She took a sip of the wine.

"Hmm, that's nice. No, what I meant was, tell me about how she was later. We met so long ago, I wondered what happened to her. Did she marry? Was she happy? Oh no, she can't have done, your name wouldn't have been Robertson, would it? That was silly of me, I'm sorry."

"No, she didn't. As you say my name would have been different, wouldn't it?" He gave a short laugh. "Tricky for her to be honest – back then – not like now when nobody bats an eye. Anyway, what can I say about her? She was okay as a mum. This is hard when I don't know how much you knew about her."

Lily realised that questions were only making things more complicated, so she tried for a version of the truth. She took another drink of the wine and smiled at him. Maybe the alcohol, which she wasn't supposed to have with her medication, was to blame, but she was warming a little to this person. He can't have had it easy, being the child of an unmarried mum in the days when it carried stigma. He was late twenties, maybe thirty, she imagined, thus not much younger than Peter would have been. Despite what had happened, what she had done, his mother hadn't taken care not to land herself in the same mess again.

"I didn't know her very well at all. I only met her." She paused. "Well, just a couple of times really."

"Oh, I see, only I got the impression you'd been friends."

"Hmm, well no, I don't think we were really friends. Lily must have misunderstood."

He rubbed his hands together, an impatient gesture. "Ah right, well, not to worry. Look, I don't have a lot of time, so can we just, you know…"

She tipped her head to one side, looked at him.

"Well, okay. Your friend said that you had something, something my mum had given you. I was intrigued. She never really had much, it all belonged to him – her father – everything. She only ever had the odd bit of tatty jewellery so, why she'd give it away…" He stopped for a moment and Lily was surprised to see a flash of anger cross his face. He gathered himself. "So, anyway I was curious. What is it, what have you got?"

"It's not exactly something I've got. I've nothing to give you."

"Oh right, this is all a bloody scam, isn't it? What are you playing at? Your mate said you had something from my mum, that's the only reason for me coming to meet you, now you say you haven't – what's going on?"

Lily had raised her hand, she patted at the air in a calming gesture. "No, no, look nothing is 'going on', not exactly. It's more information really. Yes, that's it, mostly it's information and, well, when I tell you, you might want to do something about it, I don't know."

The man before her sighed and rubbed his hand across his face. "Okay, well tell me then. What is it you know or think you know?"

"Oh, there is no doubt. This is fact. I wanted to tell you about your brother."

He took in a sharp breath and she watched as colour drained from his face. His eyes were wide with shock. Of course she had expected that, but it was more, it was anger that she saw in his face, anger, and fear.

Chapter 14

Terry Robertson leaned forward, his voice was low, a hiss. Lily instinctively leaned away from him but he stared into her eyes. "I don't want to know, okay. I don't want anything to do with him. I don't want to know about him, and if he thinks that he can come along now, after all this time, when she's dead and gone and, if he thinks…" He drew a breath, blew it back through flared nostrils and wiped his hand across his face. He pointed at her now. "I don't want to know. Tell him that, tell him to go away, to never ever try to contact me again. There is nothing for him here, nothing, do you hear me?"

He pushed back the chair and began to rise. She felt afraid, his fury was barely controlled, but she had to tell him. She had thought that this might have been a sad and poignant moment, revealing the news of Peter's very existence, or delivering sad news that would destroy the hope of years. She could never have imagined this. This anger frightened her, and she wished she hadn't come.

When she spoke, her voice was broken, not much more than a croak, "He's dead." She coughed and tried again, reaching out with her hand, trying to hold him back. "I came to tell you he's dead. I didn't know, you see, until yesterday. I didn't know your mother was no longer alive and I wanted to let her know what had happened. I wanted someone besides me to know what happened to him." She felt the tears gathering on her lower lids, and wiped them away with the tips of her fingers.

He had stopped now, slid back on the wooden seat. For a little while he seemed lost for words. "Dead. He's dead? Right, well, that takes care of that then, doesn't it?"

"Don't you want to know? Don't you want to hear about him?"

"Who were you, to him? What were you?" He was calming already now, the news of Peter's death had stopped him, and he appeared curious.

"I wasn't much really. Nobody was very much to him."

"How do you mean? Were you his mother? Did he think you were?"

Lily struggled to answer, the words that she had rehearsed in her head didn't fit the scenario. "I didn't even know whether you knew about him. I thought I would be able to meet his mother, I wondered if she thought about him. I wanted to let her know what had happened. Do you see? It was just so that someone knew."

"Yes, I knew about him. She talked about him sometimes. Later, not when I was young, but later. I think she felt a bit like you, she just wanted someone else to know. Once she was ill. Look, I'm sorry, I'm sorry for just now, I jumped to a conclusion. I thought he was going to try and make contact, try and blag some money, something."

"Money, why would you think that?"

"Well," he shrugged, "it happens, doesn't it? You hear about it. I'm not short of cash, you know – now that my mum's gone and him, her father – he's in a home. Well…"

"I see. I understand, I think. No, there was nothing like that. I just thought that his family, his real family, ought to know what happened. I didn't want him to be forgotten when I was gone."

"Well, yeah now it's starting to sink in I guess it's a bit of a shock. I've known about him for a few years and, to be honest, I always wondered how I'd feel if he tried to contact us, me. You hear about it, don't you, adoption agencies helping the kids? Parents suddenly having to cope with men and women turning up."

"Yes, I see what you mean. But honestly it's nothing like that."

"Okay, look, just hold on. I need another drink and then we need to calm down; I do at any rate. Then, yes, tell me about him. It might be good after all, to know a bit anyway. Do you want another glass of wine?"

"No, I shouldn't."

"Oh, come on. Tell you what, I'll get us a couple of sandwiches. I feel bad. There was no need for me to take it out on you, you coming to try and do the right thing."

"Well, would it be awful of me to have a whisky? Just a small one. I'm not supposed to drink but I think whisky is okay, just now and then."

As he walked away Lily settled again, she dabbed at her eyes and finished the wine.

Terry came back with two plates of sandwiches, garnished with crisps and a bit of salad. He put a large whisky in front of her. She noticed that he had bought himself the same. He had been unnerved, there was no doubt. She would need to be careful now, as she told him the facts. She had come to do the right thing, for his mother, but even more for herself, and now it was time to make sure that was just what she did.

"So," Lily broke the awkward silence with the worthless word. "How much do you know?"

"I know what she told me. She had a baby, a woman took him away. There was more of course, tears sometimes, but that was it basically…"

She bent down and pulled the large brown envelope out of her bag. She laid it on the table top and placed a hand on it. "I have some things here. They are his, from when he was born. Do you want to see them?"

He nodded. "Wait though, you still haven't told me. Were you his mother?"

"No, not me."

"How do you mean, not you? Oh, okay, my mum, Carol, she was his mother, I get that. But I mean were you his other mother, the one who brought him up?" Lily shook her head.

"So, you're from the adoption agency?" There was a flair of irritation again, in his eyes. It was developing into a ludicrous question and answer session and she had to put a stop to it. The longer it went on the harder it would be to tell him the whole story.

She handed him the envelope and he peered into it, pushed his fingers inside and drew out the little bundle of items. He turned them over on the table and stroked the little plastic bracelet. 24th July. "Okay, well that's something I didn't know. Have you not got any pictures? Nothing from when he was a baby?"

Lily gulped and reached across to unfold the tiny receipt.

Terry read it. "What the hell is this?" he shook it in the air. "What the hell is this?"

"It's a receipt," she whispered.

"How do you mean? What is it a receipt for?"

She couldn't put it into words, so she sat in silence, watching as he turned it over and over in his hand and began to see the ugliness.

"Bloody hell, no I don't believe that. She wouldn't." He stopped, lifted the paper closer to his face. "Oh Christ, but *he* would!"

Chapter 15

Lily took a sip of her drink, Terry Robertson had frightened her again with the flash of temper which seemed to be just below the surface with him. When she spoke, her voice was low, "I don't know what happened, all the details. I had hoped that your mum, his mum could tell me some of it. What do you mean 'he', who is he?"

"Who is he? Are you serious? I thought you were the one doing the telling. You're not making much sense."

The alcohol and emotion had confused Lily and she had fallen into her own trap. Her mind spun and there was only one way for her to extricate herself. "I've lied to you."

Terry Robertson put down his drink and placed his hands on the table, fingers linked. He leaned towards her. His face was impassive but his eyes were narrowed and there was fire there. "Look, I've had enough of this messing about. I've had enough of this back and forth. Either tell me why you're here, straightforward and honest, or just bugger off and leave me alone."

"Yes, I will."

"Right, we'll do it this way. I will ask you questions and you will answer, okay?"

She nodded at him and took another mouthful of the whisky.

"First of all – is this all true? Are you here because of my brother? If you're not, then you're either sick or criminal, and you don't strike me as the sort of person who would be criminal." He shrugged. "Can't bloody tell these days."

"I promise you that I am here about Peter. That was what he was called, Peter."

"Right. So, what were you to him?"

"I held him. I cared for him for just a few days."

"Then where did he go? You passed him on, yeah? You passed him on to his new parents? And did you get money for him as well?" She shook her head again and whispered.

"He died. Then, right at the start, when we had him. He died when he was just a few days old. We were heartbroken, I promise you we did all that we could." As the lie left her lips she saw it for what it was and cast it aside. "No, that's not true. We should have done more. We were so afraid, you see. It was different back then. Attitudes were so different. Like with you, your mother not being married. As you say, it doesn't matter anymore. We were afraid and we didn't do enough, and he died."

"Because you bought him? Because you didn't do it legally, you and your husband is that it, is that what you were scared of?"

"I'm not married. We were never married."

"Right, well I suppose that was a complication, but still. How did he die?"

"He had what I think was probably gastroenteritis and something called sepsis. He was so very young, you see, so little. I've read about it since. It was unbelievably quick, before we knew what was happening he was gone."

"So, how come we didn't know – well, not me, obviously – how come my mum didn't know what had happened? There must have been an inquest. How could you hide it then?"

Lily blew out her cheeks. "There wasn't an inquest, nothing like that. We didn't tell anyone what had happened."

Terry frowned. He pushed back in the chair, glanced around the pub. "I know things were different back then, but it's not all that long ago. I still don't believe you. I don't believe you could do this, hide the death of a baby. No. You're not telling me the truth, are you?"

"I am. It was wrong, it has tormented me forever, it was so wrong but it's true."

"And your husband, partner, whatever, he just went along with this?"

"She."

"Sorry?"

"My partner was a woman. That was one of the reasons, you see. We couldn't draw attention to ourselves. We couldn't risk it."

"My God." He gave a short bark of a laugh. "Well, this is a turn up, isn't it? I think I begin to see. Oh, you were ahead of your time, weren't you? That poor little sod. So, to save yourselves the embarrassment, you lied. That must have been quite a cover-up. Huh, I don't know how much to believe you now. Look, where is he? I'm going to go and see. Tell me where he is and once I see his grave, or whatever, then I'll believe you. It doesn't really make much difference, but now, now I know about him, I want to see. So, where is he?"

The silence grew and stretched. Lily felt her heart begin to pound. The pain came forward from the place it was held by the magic of medication, and she felt the world tip and withdraw as weight came down upon her chest.

Chapter 16

Lily thrust her hand into the pocket of her jacket and dragged out a small spray bottle. She puffed some of the liquid under her tongue. Terry had half risen from his chair but when he saw that she was handling the situation, he perched on the seat edge, watching, and waiting. She began to breathe more easily.

"Are you okay? Do you need an ambulance?"

She shook her head. "I'm alright. I'll be alright in just a minute."

"It's a mess this. I have to go anyway, I've got an appointment. What are we going to do?"

"You go, just go, it's fine."

"But what about him?" He lifted the little baby bracelet. "What about Peter?"

Lily shook her head. "I can't, I can't do any more today. Maybe it's best if I write it all down for you. Yes, that's going to be best, isn't it? I'll write it all down for you, calmly."

"I don't think so. Once you go, there's no guarantee for me. You've started this now. You must finish it. I want to know what happened. And, if it was him, if her father was the one behind all this, if he sold…" He paused. "If he sold that baby, Carol's baby, then I'll make him pay. He's not getting away with that, it's just a bridge too far, on top of everything else the old bastard has done."

Lily rubbed at her chest and frowned. "I don't know enough to answer that. I had hoped that I could find out the things that I always wondered about. I thought we could have talked, me and your mother. It was stupid. I see that now, but my partner Charlotte has just died and, I'm not well and I wanted to know, and I wanted to try and put some things right."

"Charlotte, were you both called Charlotte then? That's a coincidence."

"Lily, I'm Lily. I didn't meet your mother, she wouldn't have known my name, that's why I did that. Charlotte was my partner, she brought him home. I don't know anything about how she found him."

"Oh, you're quite a one for the lying aren't you, Lily? I'll say this, if I can prove that old swine, Carol's father, did this to his own grandson, then it's all going to come out, I'm going to see to that."

"What's his name?"

"Clive."

"Ah, I see. So…the signature."

"Where do you live? Maybe if I came to your house, you know, somewhere calmer."

"I don't live in Bath, I think I told you. I travelled on the train today. I live in Southsea."

"Right, so why don't I come? You can take me then?"

"Take you?"

"Yes, we'll go and see where he is. His grave or whatever, the rose garden, if that's where you put him. You can show me what else you've got, pictures and so on, and then I'm going to go and confront that old sod."

She couldn't let this happen. It was so very different from what she had imagined. His mother might have understood. She had been part of the deception after all, but Terry was innocent of any of the wrongdoing. If he was willing to confront his grandfather, in spite of the old man being sick, then what would he do when he knew the truth? She was afraid now, truly afraid. They would drag her through the courts, send her to jail, maybe. No, this couldn't happen.

"I don't want that I don't think. I'm sorry but I just want to go home now, and then I'll write it all down and send it to you. Give me your address?"

"Tell you what, you just tell me where he is, so I can go and visit. Then write the rest of it down, all you know."

"You don't need to go, do you? Why don't I get you a picture – of where he is?"

"Well, that's an idea, but actually I'd much rather go myself. I can't pretend I've ever felt much for him, not until now, but the poor little bugger had a rotten deal, and we had the same mum. No, I'll go. Where is he?"

"It's so long ago. I'm not sure I can really tell you."

"So, how were you going to take a picture then? More lies, Lily, yet more lies?"

She was backed into a tight space of her own making, rat in a trap. Her heart clenched again, reminding her that time was short.

"He's at my home. Peter is at my home."

"Oh, okay. So, ashes then. Will you let me have them? I can bury them where mum is. That would be good…" He stopped as she began yet again to shake her head.

"Don't bully me. This isn't what I had expected to happen, I can't think."

"Okay, look, give me your address, let me come to you. Let's have a day or two and then I'll come down to Portsmouth. We can meet somewhere or I can come to where you live. You decide. I'll ring you. Day after tomorrow." He glanced at his watch. "I have to go, I really do. You think about it all, write down what you can remember and then, I'll call you. In the end, you've done the right thing, you really have. Let's allow things to cool off a bit, yeah?"

Lily nodded at him, she welcomed the chance to think things through. "Yes, that's alright, yes. Just one thing though, before you go." He paused, half-turned towards the door, waited for her to continue. "Why would he do that? Your grandfather, why do you think he was involved?"

"Maybe I'll explain, maybe not. It's complicated." And he left.

Lily sat for a while longer, had another cup of coffee and then, when she felt strong enough, she left the pub. It had gone wrong, most of it had got away from her. She would ignore his calls, he couldn't find her, she would leave it, let it rest.

Chapter 17

Lily tossed and turned and didn't sleep. She was out of bed at two in the morning, making tea, pacing back and forth in the cold kitchen. Too late she understood that she should never have gone down this route. The dreadful secret had been held for decades, there had been no need to bring it into the light. She had done it only for herself, to salve her own conscience and to cross the remaining 't's before it was all over.

Now though, there was Terry Robertson. More than that there was Clive, the evil that he had been a party to. Sold his own grandson, that's what Terry had said.

She was desperately tired, could barely keep her eyes open, but the bedroom did not tempt her. She didn't want to use the wide bed, where she still slept on what had always been 'her own side'. The dark shapes that moved in the darkness, as the moon snaked its silver light between the curtains, were no longer soothing shadows, they leered and threatened her drowsy eyes. It was no longer the friendly space of past years. She gazed through the window at the garden and found no comfort in darkened trees and the wall, black and blank, like the end of the world.

The cellar was in total darkness of course, but she lit one of the tiny candles, and the light guided her down the stairs. If she could open the grave, take out the contents. What would there be? The box would have rotted surely. Would there be strands of the blanket, tiny bird-like bones, a pathetic skull, like something that you would find in a museum? After all these years, there couldn't be much left.

She could take them out and dispose of them more kindly. Put them in the garden perhaps. Fashion a little grave, tell Terry Robertson that they had been unable to bear the thought of the baby alone in the cemetery.

That would paint them in a better light. He would know, probably, that even doing that without permission was wrong. But maybe it would soften his attitude, and then she would have accomplished at least a part of her task. He'd know where his brother was and could take him away.

She looked around. It was a dreadful space, mouldy and damp and if he saw this, he would think of it as nothing other than what it was, a hiding place for their crime. The thought of bringing him here, down the old stairs and watching his anger and horror, yes, probably horror, unnerved her.

As night gave way to the overcast, cold day she opened the shed, and brought out the border spade.

In less than five minutes, she had to acknowledge that it was useless. Together, all that time ago, they had struggled to break through the earthen floor, and hollow the space. Now, alone, so much older, and frail, she was perched, panting and in pain on the narrow ledge before she had even taken out one small spadeful.

She clambered back upstairs. The world outside was wide awake by this time, bustling through the day. Lily was divorced from it all. Her existence was focused totally on Peter and her disintegrating life. She looked at the bottle of pills on the worktop. It would be an answer. She tipped a few onto the table. Her fingers reached and touched the pile of tablets. She didn't know what they would do. They were to calm her down, that would work surely. If she took them all then she would drift away, calm and unafraid. Should she write a note? Should she explain about Peter? The grave? How would she be found? She would lie on the settee, listen to the world outside and drift into whatever was next, or, as she really believed, simply cease to be.

She took the medicine and a glass of brandy into the lounge, and put them carefully on the side table. She moved aside the stuff that had been left there. It was the booklet from the funeral directors, the information about funerals and cremation. She flipped through it. The photographs of the cemetery spoke to her maudlin mood. The crematorium, floral tributes, coffin choices. She had done all this such a short while ago and now she would hand the task over to someone else.

Possibly Charlotte Mary's nephew, who was the only family there was left, would arrange things. All she had was left to him after all, and it was a sizeable legacy. The house, money, shares, everything they had accumulated. Yes, he would do it. If he forgave them for Peter. She would write that in her note, ask him to arrange things. The pictures of the urns reminded her of duties undone. But why did it matter? If Charlotte Mary's ashes were not collected, then presumably they would be disposed of somewhere. Sprinkled on a flowerbed or something.

The idea sneaked in under the planning. One minute it wasn't there and then, suddenly it was. Terry Robertson had wanted to take the ashes to his mother's grave. Peter's ashes. There were no ashes, not for Peter. She turned the booklet in her hand. The enormity of what she was thinking turned her stomach over. Why not, what difference would it make to anyone? Charlotte Mary was gone anyway, Carol Robertson wouldn't know. Peter wouldn't care. It would affect no-one but her and Terry.

She paced back and forth, struggling with thoughts that crowded at one another. It would compound the first evil, surely. But then it would put Terry Robertson's mind at rest. Whatever there was between him and his grandfather was not her concern, and anyway she could do little to help with that. His grandfather, the spectre of this man, the man who had sold his grandchild, it wouldn't be denied. This was not what she had expected and it was becoming more and more difficult to push it aside.

Chapter 18

There were many sites advertising containers for ashes, and suggested disposal methods. Fireworks, your remains could become a firework! Lily found it surprising there were so many options. Though it was fascinating, and though she knew that Charlotte Mary would have made amusing comments and inappropriate jokes, she simply searched quietly. She ordered what she wanted, with delivery the next day. A short telephone call to the funeral director organised the collection of Charlotte Mary's remains.

When Terry rang, she put him off until Monday. She needed the weekend. Time to breathe, to plan, and to give due deference to the loathsome task in front of her.

Later in the afternoon she walked to the place, slowly, remembering how she had chosen to walk on the day of Charlotte Mary's funeral: trudging slowly through drizzly rain, something ordinary to anchor her against something enormous.

The reception desk was attended by a girl she hadn't met before, and that suited her mood. She wanted to be anonymous, invisible. They ordered a taxi to take her home, it was too far to walk both ways, and the parcel was surprisingly weighty. She had been suffering many more incidents of shortness of breath, more of the clutching pain, and needed the spray often.

She knew that she should make an appointment with the doctor, discuss her options. There had been talk of some sort of surgery, more drugs. But she didn't want it. She didn't want the waiting around in hospitals and clinics, the enforced discussions, and she didn't want to make any more decisions. She had no great desire to hang on to a life that had become so very dull, so ordinary.

The box was inside a blue plastic bag and she didn't look at it, not until she was home. It was just a plain thing. Charlotte Mary's name and dates were on a small label. She placed it on the sideboard. For a while she stared at it. She didn't know how to feel. Here it was, all that was left of the brilliance, the beauty and the huge ego that had been her partner for decades. She had expected to cry, but her eyes were dry. She had expected sadness, grief. There was nothing, just a sort of numbness. It puzzled her, and she had to face the fact that her feelings for Charlotte had been diluting gradually for years and it was only habit, and laziness, and of course fear, that had held them together. What a waste. What a dreadful waste.

Sitting as it did on the polished wood, the effect was too much like an altar, so in the end she pushed it into the china cabinet, closed the door and climbed upstairs to bed. She was worn out. She took two of the pills that she was only ever supposed to take singly and crawled under the covers. In minutes, she was asleep.

* * *

The delivery was early and the driver handed over the parcel with a bright smile. Lily watched him drive away, and stood gazing down the road long after he had turned at the junction. So often these days she found herself slowed almost to a standstill. Staring for minutes at a time, at bubbles in the washing up water or watching water flow into the washbasin as her hands dripped onto the bathroom floor.

"Morning, Lily. How are you?" The woman from the house next door paused on the way past the gate. "I've been meaning to come round. See how you're doing. If you need anything, anything at all, you know where we are. Please, give us a call or just come to us, come and knock on the door. If the lights are on, you'll know we're in. You must come for supper sometime soon, or maybe lunch."

"Thank you. Yes, lovely, thank you." She backed into the hall, slammed the door, shut out the world.

After tearing away the padded bag and the plastic wrap, she held the contents in her hand, turning it back and forth. It was a nice thing, the little blue urn. It had a lid to screw off and the image of a white bird on the side of it. She imagined it was a dove. She sighed. He should have had something like this, shouldn't he? Tears came then. No, he shouldn't have had something like this at all, what he should have had was a life. She felt the anger building, it took her breath away and she had to sit down, until the dizziness abated.

* * *

She laid a fresh white cloth on the kitchen table and placed the blue ceramic container on top. Inside the crematorium box was a transparent plastic bag. It was sealed. There was quite a lot, more than she had expected and it was obvious immediately that it was more than the blue urn would hold.

She went to the kitchen, fetched the scissors, and a dessert spoon. Briefly she wondered what she would do with the leftovers, the extra ashes. She tipped her head to one side – how very strange it all was.

Chapter 19

Lily unscrewed the lid of the blue urn. Inside was white and smooth. She opened the box and sheared off the closure of the plastic bag. She spread open the top and then, so that there would be adequate access for the spoon, folded it down, rolled over the edges. Charlotte Mary had been colourful, a bird of paradise, a humming bird, exuberant and flashy. And here were her remains, grey, dull sand, a few small clumps mixed among the grains. Lily leaned her face closer to the table. There was no smell, nothing, it was all very bland.

She reached in, poked with her index finger at the surface. It left a small indentation. She rubbed some of it together between her finger tips. Gritty.

What had it all been about? The rebellion, the passion, the pain. It was all so very pointless, if this is what it came down to.

The sound of gentle knocking on the kitchen door made her jump. The handle rattled. Through the small glass pane, she saw the face of Sandra from next door. Middle-aged, kind, sometime plant waterer and receiver of parcels, holder of the spare keys. Sandra and Bob moved in just a few years ago, so they were never lied to, never misled about the relationship. She was waving and smiling.

Lily pulled a tea towel from the rail and laid it over the items on the table. "Hello, Sandra. What can I do for you?"

"I felt bad, this morning, when I saw you. Afterwards, I realised it seemed that I was just, well you know, saying something because I'd seen you. It wasn't that at all. I really meant it. We have been thinking about you. I wonder if you'd like to come now and have tea? I have made a cake, I know you always liked my carrot cake." She laughed. "Well, you always said you did."

"That's kind of you but..."

The other woman reached out, grasped Lily's hand. "Lily, don't mind me saying it, but you don't look well. Not surprising really but... come on, come. Just for half an hour, have a cup of tea, some cake. It's not good for you, in here on your own. I've hardly seen you out at all. It must be hard, we know how long you'd been together. Even though she'd been ill, it must be hard." She was pulling at Lily now, she threw an arm around her shoulder. "Come on, just for half an hour?"

It was easier to go than to fight, so, with a glance towards the table, Lily allowed herself to be dragged outside.

Sandra's house smelled of baking. It was warm and welcoming, and as Lily leaned against soft cushions on the couch she felt an overwhelming urge to cry. Her life had become so dark, so very desperate, that this home was less of a comfort and more of a taunt.

She accepted the plate loaded with cake, nodded, smiled, and murmured responses to Sandra's questions and harmless chatter, and she experienced it all as if from a great distance. She thought about the table in her own kitchen, she wished that she had taken the way out, and that she no longer existed.

Sandra was kneeling in front of her. *When did that happen?* "Oh, you poor love." There was moisture on her cheeks and Lily realised that her hand was shaking. Sandra took away the plate and slid onto the settee. She wrapped Lily in a gentle hug. "Have you seen the doctor, are you getting any help? It's no shame to ask for help."

Lily pulled away, wiped at her face with the napkin. "No, no, I'm alright. Really, I am, it's just now and then, you know. I am so sorry, making a fool of myself like this. I'm sorry."

"Don't apologise. It's me who should be doing that. We've neglected you."

"No, really. It's fine. I'm no company anyway. Please, I think I'd like to go home."

"Stay, eat your cake, rest for a while." Sandra picked up the plate and held it out.

"No, no, I'm sorry, I have to go. I just have to go." Lily pushed up from the couch and rushed towards the door. "I'm sorry Sandra, you've been kind. I just can't do this now. I am so sorry."

Back in her own house she slammed the door, turned the lock, and then ran into the front room to drag the curtains across the window.

She threw herself onto the settee, drew up her knees, curled into a ball and gave in to the wails and sobs that had skulked in her soul for thirty years.

Exhaustion brought her some small relief with a couple of hours of sleep. When she woke, it was the middle of the afternoon. She went into the kitchen and poured a mug of milk. Standing by the window she had her drink and then turned to look at the table. The strange bumps under the tea cloth. She had to do this now. Terry Robertson would come on Monday, and she had to be ready for him.

She didn't give herself time to think again. She dug the spoon into the contents of the polythene bag and spooned them carefully into the urn.

Chapter 20

The contents of Charlotte Mary's box were depleted, but it wasn't empty. Lily replaced the container in the china cupboard.

She took the small urn into the living room and stood it on the coffee table. She brought out one of the votive candles, and a glass holder, and lit the wick. The brave little flame quivered now and then in a passing draught, but burned bright and true as the light in the room faded.

Slowly it came to her that she had pulled a veil across the facts, already she was thinking of this small, blue jar as Peter's. It wasn't, it was just another lie.

She blew out the candle, leaned back against the cushions, and closed her eyes. Maybe Sandra was right, maybe the doctor could help her. She knew that her thinking was becoming muddier, that the sharpness of her mind was more blunted than could be attributed to the effects of grief alone. She also knew that it was fear and sadness, and the ever-present guilt that were smothering her spirit, and no doctor could help her with that, because it was far, far too late.

* * *

On Saturday morning, she put the blue urn into the cupboard and then, when the walls began to close in, she walked to the seafront. She had to choose. Either she fought back, or finished it quickly with the pills that were still in a tiny heap on the table in the living room. She must not let herself go slowly with neglect and despair, she was worth more than that.

She turned to watch people strolling along the seafront, across the common. There was a sharp breeze across the pebbled beach. She stood in front of the war memorial, thought about the wasted lives. If these people had been given a second chance, they would have snatched at it and lived it until the last breath. She had been given so much more than them and on top of that the chance to do some good in the last days.

She followed her usual route through the rose garden and then back to Palmerston Road. It had all changed, she didn't belong here, no longer went to work, no longer mixed with friends. She wasn't needed, and she wasn't loved. But she wasn't dead yet and there was still work to do.

She spent the night on the settee in the living room. Her body refused to join her spirit in the newfound resolve and any exertion brought on the pains that took her breath away. Mrs Fleming had made up the bed with fresh sheets and covers, she could snuggle into the sweet-smelling softness but, tempting as it was, upstairs was too far away, and the effort too much.

All day Sunday she spent under the blanket in the downstairs room. She left the curtains closed and moved from the settee only to visit the downstairs toilet, or to heat some water and pour it onto powder to make lemon tea.

She drowsed through the day and by evening she was stronger. She was determined to be ready for Monday when Terry Robertson would come, and she would take her part in the next act of the shadow play that was her life.

* * *

He didn't come until after lunch and Lily had spent much of the morning looking through the window and even, on one occasion, standing at the front door, peering back and forth. She washed her hands and face and dressed in a plain skirt and sweater. She combed her hair, put away the blankets, and tidied up in the living room.

He arrived when she was in the kitchen drinking a cup of tea and eating biscuits. The biscuits were a little stale but the sweetness was kind to her depleted body, and she felt better. He was dressed very much as he had been for their meeting in Bath, but had on a wool hat. He snatched it off as she opened the door and waved an arm behind her, silently inviting him inside.

"Terry. Did you have a good journey?"

"Yes, it's not that far. Cold here though. I had to park down on the seafront, finding a space nearby is impossible."

"Yes, I know. I don't drive but it was always a problem for Charlotte. She used to fume about it."

"I never said, I am sorry that you lost your friend. Well, partner. It must be hard for you."

She couldn't answer his unexpected kindness, so she nodded and turned away.

His voice was low and quiet as he spoke again, "I want to apologise to you, I was very rough, rude, last time I saw you. You had come with good intentions, and I shouldn't have behaved the way I did. I've felt so bad since then. Even though, what your erm… what Charlotte did was wrong, that wasn't your fault, and I respect what you tried to do, letting my mum know about him – about the baby."

She couldn't meet his eyes, and turned from the door and walked into the living room where she had placed the urn, again, on the low table in front of the settee.

77

He stopped as he walked through the door, his eyes on the blue jar. "Oh. Oh. I…"

She was shocked to see the gleam of moisture in his eyes. He took a few steps forward and cleared his throat and then paused, unsure of what to do next. Lily sat in the chair next to the fire and Terry perched on the edge of the settee.

After a few moments, he reached towards the table. "May I?"

He glanced at Lily and she nodded. Her heart was racing and she felt sick.

He picked up the urn carefully, in both hands, and drew it towards him. "It looks new, it looks very new. You must have taken great care of it, for all this time."

Chapter 21

Lily pointed to the cabinet in the corner.

"It was in the cupboard," she said. Not a lie, not the truth.

Terry nodded. He spoke again, quietly, almost reverentially, "I thought it would be different. Something like you see in films, fancy, old-fashioned, and a bit silly really, if you know what I mean?" Lily nodded. "Only, this is nice," he continued, "well, maybe that's the wrong word but, you know, it's... well, appropriate I suppose." He continued to hold it, his thumb stroked the little white bird on the side. His next question startled her. "Is it sealed?"

"Sealed?" she repeated.

"Yes, did they put something round the lid, to seal it? I don't know about these things. Obviously if you're going to – you know – scatter them it wouldn't be, but keeping it?" He shrugged, but in the absence of an answer he was pressed to continue. "If they know you're going to keep it, do they seal it with something?"

She swallowed, tried to moisten her mouth before she could answer. She thought of the plastic bag, but that wasn't quite the same, was it? "I don't know. Whether they do that. Seal them." Again, she had spoken the truth but on her lips it became a lie.

They sat in uncomfortable silence, Lily was the one who broke it. "Tell me about her."

"My mum?"

"Yes, Charlotte was the one who was in contact with her. I always thought she met her. What you told me about your grandfather – Clive. Well, it makes me wonder if even that was a mistake. On my part, I mean. Maybe I jumped to conclusions."

Terry took a minute to think before he answered. "She was okay as a mum. I always had stuff to eat. I had decent clothes. She wasn't the sort who would come to the school, to plays and things. She never did much of that. She was… shy. She didn't mix."

Lily could tell that he was feeling awkward, didn't want to do this, but she pressed on. It was a snowball and now it was rolling, it wouldn't stop. "So, your own father?"

"What about him?"

"Who was he, he wasn't the same as…?" She pointed at the urn. Terry looked down, seemed only now to remember that he still had it on his lap, held gently between his curled fingers.

He placed it on the coffee table, and shook his head. "No. He wasn't."

"What was he like?"

"He wasn't, a father – not ever. I didn't know him. I only know what I was told. My mum, she ran away from home at one stage, and it was during that time that she met the bloke who got her pregnant with me. When he found out she was pregnant, he went back to his wife. She tried to make a go of it on her own. She tried really hard I think. Struggled to keep going. But she hadn't got much education, no real qualifications and in the end, he, Clive, found her and made her go back to Bath. That was before I was born. She lived there with her own mum, Granny, and me.

"They'd always had property, some of it had been in the family for a long time, and he was clever. The boom in the sixties and seventies had made him rich, he bought more and more. Yes, to give him his due he did okay at that. In the end, he even converted the house in Southcote Place into flats and bought a different place for us to live, more modern. Granny was dead, my mum was ill by then and not long after we moved, Clive had a stroke. She couldn't look after him and there was no bloody way I was going to. So, he's in a nursing home."

"Oh, I thought Alzheimer's, dementia."

Terry shook his head. "No, not that. He's lost a lot of movement and his speech is not that easy to understand sometimes but, up to now anyway, he still knows what's going on. They even tell me he's improving. I go now and then, business stuff, that's all."

"Right. Do you intend to ask him about the baby?"

Before he answered Terry slid back on the settee, sat more comfortably. "Oh, I'm going to do a lot more than ask him."

It wasn't said kindly and Lily hesitated, but in the end, she had to ask for more. As they talked she felt her interest build, she felt more alive than she had for days. She was encouraged by the idea that maybe there was still a chance to find out about Peter, a little of the story anyway.

"You really think he was the one who sold the baby?"

"Yes. I do. My mum, oh, she had her faults, I've never pretended anything different. She was weak and she used stuff: drink, sometimes drugs. She was a mess a lot of the time, but she wouldn't have done that. Not if she'd had any choice. She kept me, didn't she? She did what she could to look after me."

"Yes, but so did he though, Clive, I mean. He didn't do the same thing with you, did he? He didn't sell you."

"No, he didn't. I'm still trying to process all of it. I'm confused and there are things that I don't want to think about, but I have to. I have to and I will, but slowly and with as much information as I can gather. And if I can prove it, then he'll pay. At the moment, we don't know enough. That note, the receipt, I recognised that signature. It wasn't my mum's and I'd know his anywhere."

"So, you'll ask him? Show him the receipt?"

Terry rubbed a hand over his face and then before he spoke he leaned forward again. "Okay, this is the thing." He pointed at the urn. "I want to try and get this tested."

"Tested?"

"Yes, DNA. Now, it's not usually very successful. I've looked into it in the past, researched the whole business but more from the usual side, people who are alive, you know? A few years ago, I thought about trying to trace the bloke that got my mum pregnant. I didn't do it, I realised there was no point." Lily nodded. "But this is different. Generally, it seems it's impossible to do it on cremated ashes. But there are one or two places that say if there are bits of bone..." He paused and looked at her. "Is this upsetting for you. Talking about it like this?"

The memory of yesterday, the transfer of the remains, brought heat to her face, but Lily shook her head and answered him. "No, no, I'm not squeamish about things like that."

"Well, there are a couple of places that reckon that if there are bits of bone, or teeth..."

Lily interrupted, "He didn't have teeth, he was new-born."

"I know, but apparently they are there in the skull, already formed. Anyway, if there is enough, these people reckon there is a chance that they can do the tests. It's a very remote chance, but I reckon I've got nothing to lose. It hinges on how the, erm..." He pointed. "How the remains have been prepared. I'm hoping that because it's a while ago, well, maybe they weren't as efficient. I don't know."

"But what do you want to find out?"

"Well, they can find out the gender, but we know that already of course, we know he was a boy. More importantly they can give a good idea about paternity. They can prove who the father is, and the mother. Even though we know that, we know about Mum, it's all part of it. It would all be evidence."

Lily covered her mouth with her hand, he didn't need to spell it out and he saw that she understood. She whispered, "You think he did that to your mum? You think her own father did that to her, had sex with her?"

Terry nodded. "I know he did. She told me before she died. But she didn't need to. I knew full well by then what he was like. Oh, I knew alright. If I can prove this, he's going to stand trial and it's all going to come out. Everything. Not for what he did to Mum, it's too late, she's gone but – well yes, okay. If it's the only way to get him, for what he did to me and then at least I can tell everyone… about this." His face was red now and as he pointed towards the table, the urn, his hands were shaking.

"Terry. Did he abuse you? Is that what you're saying? How dreadful."

"I'm not going to talk about it, not with you, not with anyone, yet. But if it turns out that we're right about this and I can prove this, well, then I'm willing to take it all to the authorities. I'll ruin his reputation. He's vain, he's always been well-known, respected. He rubbed shoulders with the great and the good. I'll shame him, for my mum, for me and for Peter and the others." His face was twisted with fury, and he had to clear his throat and try visibly to calm himself before continuing.

"I owe you my thanks. You gave me a kick up the bum. I'd made my mind up not to do anything, I thought I'd got past it, the things he did to me. I've toed the line, I still do. He's the one with the money, the property and I've kept my mouth shut, just so I could have my nice life. He owes me that, but now…" He shook his head. "It's all too much, it's the last straw that's all, it's time to make him pay. When you came and told me about this, when I saw that receipt…" He paused and thought for a moment. "I've been a coward for too long, lazy and greedy and now, it's got to end. He can't get away with it. I had thought seeing him in the wheelchair, struggling to feed himself – I thought that was enough, but it's not and so…" He fell silent and closed his eyes. He looked spent and Lily felt the stirring of her own fury on his behalf.

Chapter 22

Lily's mind was in turmoil. Here was this young man, just a little younger than Peter would have been, opening his heart. Telling her things that he hadn't told other people. He was revealing these dreadful secrets because he thought, in front of him on the table, was the evidence of such wrongdoing that he would no longer be able to turn from it. But there was a darker truth, one hidden in the gloomy room under their feet and fear won again.

"I don't know if I want to let him go," she whispered.

Terry had to lean forward. "What, what did you say?"

"I said…" She raised her voice and looked at him. "I said, I don't think I want to let him go."

"I can understand that." He was calm as he responded, he didn't see any threat to his plan, not yet.

She reached towards the table. "No, you see. I thought that you were going to bury him, with his mother. I said that I would let you take him away because that felt right. But this…" She pulled the urn towards her.

"Well, I will. I will bury him with her. I have already looked into it and it's easy to arrange, just a question of paperwork really. I will bury him with his mum."

She felt panic building and her voice sounded like a whine. "But first, this thing that you're proposing. How will that be? You'll have to send it all away, will you?" She paused, remembered Friday, the desecration, then continued. "Will you disturb him?"

"It's impossible not to, of course." He slid forward now, bending towards her. "I see that this must be hard for you. After all this time. But why did you come to Bath, if you weren't going to let him go?"

The answer was another lie, they came so quickly now. "I thought that your mother would want to have him, and I was ready for that." She hadn't been, now she saw she hadn't been. She had thought that they would open the grave, arrange to put the child to rest somewhere pleasant, a wood perhaps or secretly in a family plot. She had thought the mother might feel just as guilty as she and Charlotte Mary of wrongdoing. It had seemed logical that she would want to be a party to a plan that would keep the secrets.

In the desperate days after Charlotte Mary's funeral, with her mind in turmoil, she had acted impetuously. The plan was unravelling and becoming so much more complicated. She needed time to think. She felt the pain, building in her chest.

She leaned over and took up the little jar, held it close. "I don't think I want you to take him away."

Terry had moved towards her. "Oh, come on. You have to, you came to me, remember, you told me about this. I'd cut the very idea of him, of *my brother*, out of my life. I didn't want to know and you made me face it. It's ashes Lily. It's just his ashes. He's gone, he can't be disturbed, and then they will send it back and I promise you…" He looked deep into her eyes, his voice was low, serious. "I promise you that I will bury him with his mum and that I will take you there to see where he is. I will have his name on the headstone. His full name, Peter Robertson, we can put his birth date on, and when he died.

It will all be done properly. Now, wouldn't that be nice? His name, his memorial. Wouldn't that be better than him just here? In a cupboard, only you knowing. Isn't that what you wanted? I thought that was what you wanted. You said so. You said you came to Bath because other people should know."

"Why can't you just go to the authorities and tell them what your grandfather did. Other people have done it. Brave people have done it after years of silence. You don't need this, this is not you. This is Peter. It's a different thing."

"I've told you, haven't I? He has always ruled the roost and I've let him. I suppose I thought that if I could just hang on until he was dead, then I would get it all, everything he'd built up, all that he's worked for. I didn't want to risk losing it, so I kept my mouth shut. It wasn't just for me though. While my mum was still alive I hid what was happening with him, with me. When I was very small I was confused and frightened, when I was older I was ashamed. I knew it was wrong, but I never told her, I never told anyone. When she first told me about her other baby, she didn't say it was Clive's. She never did, and I never told her what he'd done to me, so it all stayed secret. But when I saw that paper, that receipt, I realised what it could mean. It's quite simple really, I changed my mind. I can't let him go to his grave without facing him with it. I must. If I can prove that he is the father of his own daughter's baby, and that he sold it, it will destroy him. I've got access to him, and I've got stuff left from when she died. I'm sure there must be hair, something like that in all the stuff I kept, stuff that's still at the house. And, I may be damned for it, but I want to destroy him. I want him to face what he's done, all of it. I want him to look me in the face and acknowledge all of it. Then I want them to throw him in a cell."

"But he's old. He's sick. They surely won't do that. They might decide that he's too sick. It might kill him, the trauma. What if he's not Peter's father, what if that's someone else."

"Even if it isn't him, he sold the baby, didn't he? He hid his birth and worse than that, he actually made money from it – that's just sick. But I think I'm right, I'm convinced that I'm right, and he can't get away with it. Look, let me take this away." He pointed to the ashes. "I'll keep in touch, I'll let you know what happens and afterwards I'll take you to his grave."

"I can't."

It was an impasse. Lily was afraid, Terry determined. He was the first to speak. "Look, I'm really disappointed about this, I can't pretend I'm not, but maybe there's a way around it."

She looked up at him. "How?"

"Okay, if you really don't want to let him go to Bath, to be buried with his mum – and I don't understand it, this change of mind – but, okay, if that's really how you feel, let me…" He stopped and gulped. "Let me see if I can find out how much stuff they need, how much would be enough to do the job. Then we can open the urn, take some out and send that away."

She was shaking her head. He thought he knew why, he leaned and patted her hand. "Oh, I know, I know it's a horrible thought, I know. I'll do it though. I can do it, or ask someone else. I don't know, an undertaker, that sort of person, and you'd never know. I'll seal it up afterwards and you don't have to watch. Will you agree to that?"

She wanted to help him, she really did, but this wasn't the way. These ashes would throw such confusion into the mix that she couldn't let him have them, it was as much to protect Terry as herself. She would have to sort this out, that was without doubt, but she had no idea how she was going to do it.

Chapter 23

"Let me make you a drink, a cup of tea. You need to calm down." As he spoke Terry rose from the settee, and took a step towards the living room door. "Is that okay? I'll make us both a drink and we'll sit and talk quietly. We'll work it all out. I'm sure we can come to some sort of agreement."

Lily nodded, she managed a smile. "I'll do it, you don't know where things are."

He put a hand on her shoulder. "No, it's fine, I'll manage." And he disappeared into the hall. Moments later she heard water gush from the kitchen tap, and the click and clatter of cups and cupboards.

When she had met him, she had thought Terry a disappointment. She had wanted to see Peter, her idea of how he would have been, grown and wonderful, not this ordinary person. But he wasn't ordinary at all. He carried such dreadful secrets with him, such pain and anger. And still, despite it all, here he was now in her kitchen, making a drink because she was upset, and all she had done was stand in the way of his plans.

She placed the blue urn on the table. If she had Peter's ashes to give him, then she would. If she had the means to help him in his belated quest for justice, then she would. It spoke of such strength of character that he had saved his mother, and presumably his grandmother, from pain; he had locked away his own hurt. He had even allowed his grandfather to grow old without shaming him. Yes, he admitted that the reasons were not loyalty or kindness, but he'd done it, when he believed it was his secret alone. Yet, now he saw that the injustice had spread wider than even he had believed, he was willing to face the embarrassment and anguish that disclosure would surely mean. He was a fine young man. And she couldn't help him because she was a liar, and a coward. He shamed her.

He had put the mugs onto a tray, and there was a packet of biscuits and the sugar container from the worktop. "Probably not what you're used to but here we are. Do you want sugar?"

"Thank you."

They sat quietly for a while, sipping the hot drink, until the silence became awkward. Terry glanced around. He pointed to a picture on the mantelpiece. "Is that Charlotte?"

Lily had forgotten it was there, just a framed snap of them in London that was so familiar that she didn't notice it any more. Charlotte Mary wore a bright summer dress; a shawl was draped loosely around her shoulders, and big sunglasses held back her hair. Lily stood beside her, a little less flamboyantly dressed, but smiling. They had their arms around each other. "Yes, London, a book fair. We were in publishing. It was fun. That was a good day."

He put down his mug and walked over. "She was lovely looking. Well, you both were of course, but she is striking."

"Yes, she used to turn heads."

"Was this after? After Peter?"

"No, it was just before. Not long before, now I think of it."

"Why did you do it? I mean, you could have had a baby, one of you. That's what people do, isn't it?"

"Ah, it was different back then – everything. It was her, just her. I was never a part of it. Not until he came."

"Oh, that's odd though, isn't it?"

"It was typical of her. She was…" Lily thought for a moment. "She was spontaneous and selfish, she was very spoilt, used to having anything and everything she wanted. She'd had an affair, and I think she saw this as some sort of glue to stick us back together. She didn't talk to me about it, just went ahead and did it. Brought him home. It would have been wonderful. I think we could have sorted out all the paperwork and what have you, given time. She would have fixed that, and then we would have had him, a son. Yes, it would have been wonderful."

"It's tragic. How long did he live? After she brought him home, how long did you have him?"

"Just a few days. It's hard to say exactly, we were in such a panic, the hours ran into each other, and then he died."

"Do you think, if he'd stayed with his mum, he would still be alive now? I mean, was he already ill when she brought him?"

"He could have picked up the infection as soon as he was born. But of course, I am only guessing at a lot of it. We didn't even take him to a doctor. At the time, we thought we couldn't, but that was wrong, so very wrong, it was shameful. It's what we should have done. What his mum would have done. So, the answer has got to be yes. If he hadn't been sold, then he would very possibly still be alive. We are all responsible. We stole his life, all of us."

"Yes. You should have got him help, but it's all too late. There's no point tormenting yourself with it."

"He might still have died anyway. It's very serious, what I believe was wrong with him. Anyway, that was how it was. We were devastated. I'd come to love him so much. I didn't think I'd ever get over it. I don't think I have."

"So, will you let me find out his history? You said that was what you wanted. Let me find out who his father was, well, maybe – perhaps it will just prove who his father wasn't, and we have to be prepared for that as well. Let me fill in some of the blanks. You owe him that, don't you?"

"I can't. I just can't." And then, she saw that she could, that she must. There were going to be consequences, everything could be laid bare and her life, the life she knew, would be over. But this life, as she was now, wasn't worth preserving was it. If she did this thing, helped Peter's brother, at least that would put some of it right again.

She swallowed, once she set this in motion there was no going back. Terry sat before her, admirable, hopeful. She would help him. "If you had something else? If you had something instead of just ashes, wouldn't that be better?"

"How do you mean, something else?"

"What if you had hair? Hair or… something else?"

"Have you got a lock of his hair? That would be wonderful. That would be perfect."

"You'll have to give me time. I can't give it to you now, not right now." The excitement left his eyes.

She continued the lie. "We have a safety deposit box. Charlotte was always afraid of fire, floods. A few years ago, there were floods. A lot of the houses in Southsea were inundated. We just put all the precious things in it. Papers, things like that." She stopped short of saying the words, of telling him that there was a lock of hair from the baby in this non-existent box. She eased her guilty soul by not verbalising the untruth.

"So, you'd let me have it?"

"I could let you have some. You don't need much, do you?" As she spoke part of her mind was in the basement with the dreadful grave.

"So, what shall we do? How will we do this?"

"I'll go to the bank. I'll call you."

"We could go now. I could take you."

"No, no. I can't, not now, not today." She flopped back against the chair and closed her eyes.

"Okay, okay. I'm sorry, I didn't mean to pressure you. It's just that it's better than I could have hoped."

"I think you should go now. I need to lie down. I'll call you, when I have it."

"Tomorrow?"

"Maybe tomorrow. Yes, or the day after."

When he had gone, Lily went down to the basement. The old spade was still there, leaning against the wall. She dragged it to the dark corner and jabbed at the floor. There was so little impression she had to bend close with her torch to see the tiny marks. Maybe if she scraped at it, maybe if she just scraped away with a small trowel, she could get in.

Chapter 24

She went upstairs and sat before the dressing table mirror. With only the dim light from the landing behind her, she looked like a wraith. A vague, rather bedraggled woman with hollow eyes and a downturned, lipless mouth stared out at her. She lifted a hand and touched her hair. If he had only wanted a keepsake, that would have worked. She would clip a curl, from the back where the colour was still true. Tie a piece of old ribbon around it and send him on his way. But that wasn't the answer. It wouldn't be very long before he was back, calling out the deception.

She lay on top of the bed and closed her eyes. Sleep wouldn't come. The day played and replayed behind her lids. After an hour, she gave up and plodded back down and into the kitchen.

Under the sink, in the cupboard that held dusters, candles, and a couple of old brushes, there was a small trowel. She took it along with the big flashlight and went down into the cellar.

The feeble light from the bulb above the stairs seemed brighter to her night-time eyes, but as she turned the corner she switched on the torch. She placed it on the floor, the beam shining towards the wall and pooling over the uneven surface of the grave.

She jabbed at the crust of soil with the point of the trowel. Without the weight of the spade adding to the strain she was able to manage better. She had to stop often to catch her breath, and her arms quivered with the unaccustomed activity. Eventually she had chipped away enough so that there was a small place where the soil was softer. She scraped and scratched at it until there was a pile of the dark earth beside her.

The hole was small but she had never intended to open more than was necessary. She had already determined it would be beyond her, and anyway she didn't want to see. Several times her stomach lurched when she thought of what she was doing, and tears flowed across her cheeks over and over. She wiped them away with the back of her dirty hands and the hem of her sweater.

The change in sound, and the feel of it, as the tool bit into the ground, was minimal, but she saw that splinters of wood were mixed with the soil. Lily picked up some of the detritus and rubbed it between her fingers. She moved towards the light and held some of the dirt in the yellow cone. It was unmistakable, there was wood now. It was crumbly and dark.

Her knees began to quiver and she fell onto her backside. She had known it was there, of course she had, it had tormented her from the first day. Now, looking at the tiny slivers of the box, the reality of it all was overwhelming. She was shivering. She was overcome with grief yet again, just as raw as on the day that he had died.

She could go no further. She laid down the trowel and, bracing against the wall, struggled to her feet. She climbed the stairs on her hands and knees and staggered into the kitchen. Sitting at the kitchen table she sipped at a glass of brandy, and waited until her pounding heart slowed, and the pain in her chest eased.

If she allowed herself too long to think about it then, she knew, she would lose her nerve. She must make her mind a blank. Like plunging live crabs into pots of boiling water, she must do this quickly and not consider the detail.

She fished about in the sewing box until she found a tiny plastic bag. It contained a spare button from Charlotte Mary's last winter coat. She emptied it, and then looked back in the box and pulled out a length of blue ribbon. It wasn't old enough, so she rubbed her dirty fingers back and forth across it to dull the brightness and take away the sheen. There were thin rubber gloves in a box in one of the kitchen drawers and she pulled them out. She began to push her fingers into them and then she stopped. No, if she was to do this then the least she could do was to be honest about it. She would lay her hands on him.

She took the tiny embroidery scissors from the sewing kit, and then sat for a moment with all the things before her on the table. She bowed her head. She felt that if she could pray, if there was something, some higher power to believe in, then now would be the time to call on that faith for strength and courage. But of course, any higher power, even a vengeful God, could never look kindly on what she was about to do.

She went back to the top of the stairs. "I'm sorry, I'm so sorry," she spoke to the empty darkness and then made her way back to the corner of the basement, where the tiny mound of earth witnessed the desecration of the poor, sad grave.

Chapter 25

Lily's fingers probed the dark space. She could feel it, a different texture from the surrounding earth. It surprised her that the box had survived as well as it had, for all these lonely years. The gap she had made was slightly too near the wall and it took more of her failing strength to correct the error, but she dug on. When her breathing became too laboured and the pains overwhelmed her, she rocked back onto her heels and rested. Her legs and knees stiffened and cramped but the top corner of the box was under her fingers, so she drove herself on.

There was more work necessary on the hole before it was large enough to allow access to the flat top of the box. Lily shone the torch downwards. Now, with the point of the trowel she dug and scraped and jabbed and the wood splintered, and then finally, she felt the resistance yield. She climbed painfully back to the kitchen and grabbed a sharp knife from the drawer. This was a better tool to pick at the edges, until there was room to insert her index and middle fingers and her thumb.

In her mind's eye, she pictured the little nest they had made for him. Soft towels and a folded cloth to lay his head upon. When she felt it, she cried out in anguish and jerked her hand back into her lap, where she rubbed and rubbed at her fingers. She gulped and shuddered in the darkness but then she thought of Terry, and she drew in a great breath and reached again into the miniature coffin. She had closed her eyes. It wasn't possible to see what she was doing anyway, and in some ways, this was easier. She could feel the roundness of the tiny skull, not crumbled to dust then, not yet. He'd had hair, a surprising amount of it really. Dark it had been, and they had stroked at it with a soft brush, playing with him as if he were a little doll. She thought she could feel it between her fingers but there was no way that she would be able to cut it one handed, so she tugged gently. It came away with no resistance at all and when she held her fingers under the light of the torch she saw a clump of fine strands.

Peter.

Would it be enough? Probably, but how would she convince Terry that it was what she had kept of a living child, or even from one recently dead? Surely you would cut a proper lock, small as that would have been. These sad strands were not enough to be tied with the ribbon. But then, they didn't need to be did they? She had said she would give him some, it would be unreasonable for him to expect to take away all of such a precious keepsake.

Holding her breath, she picked up the small plastic bag and rubbed it open. She pushed the few hairs inside and quickly pressed the two edges together, sealing it.

She crawled to the wall and sat with her back against the cold bricks, her eyes closed, and her insides quivering and roiling. She had done it.

Back in the kitchen she examined the bag and the contents; she hoped it would be enough. There was more than it had seemed in the dreadful moments after she had retrieved them – there would be no need to try to fetch any more. Would it be suitable? She saw that, pulling as she had, the hair was attached to matter that she didn't want to think about. Not much, but enough to thicken the ends and make a few of them clump together. She could clean it. The idea appalled her. It seemed that every way she turned another wall rose before her, another complication. She drank a glass of water and, now, before she let it become a torment, she went back again into the cellar.

She looked into the hole and realised that if she were to simply scrape the soil back in, it would fall into the coffin, onto the child. She went to the bedroom. There was a tiny bowl there, an antique china thing, and it was small enough.

She lowered it into the grave and wedged it tightly above the hole in the wood, and then scraped the soil back in. She placed the candleholder onto the newly disturbed surface and, watching the gentle flame, she murmured, "I would never have done it, never have disturbed you sweetheart but he is so brave, your brother. So very brave and I know that you want me to help him. I wish you could have met him. Sleep soundly, precious."

It was over and, despite the anguish, there was a feeling of success and oddly, optimism. Though it could end up a disaster for her, at least, in some way, Peter would be remembered and surely that was the whole reason for starting down this road in the first place.

She turned on her computer and began research into the sites offering advice about DNA testing. It wasn't long before she was convinced that the hair, attached to the minute amounts of skin – or whatever it was – would work better than hair alone, which would be almost worthless. So, she would give him this. If he asked about the strange appearance of it, she would tell him that she didn't know. That it had always been that way, that it had been wrapped in silk, tied with a ribbon. That she had never examined it closely, that it was too awful to do that. She would say that Charlotte Mary had taken it from the baby just before they had buried him, and hope that his desire to avoid upsetting her would preclude too many probing questions.

She was tiptoeing forward and trusting in fate, and karma, and luck and how Charlotte Mary would have laughed at the mess she was in just because she had tried to do the right thing.

It was a long time before her nerves began to settle. She paced through the house, lifting the bag over and over and peering at the contents. Eventually though, exhaustion overtook her and she drifted into an uneasy sleep.

Woken after just a few hours by the birds and the noise of cars and children and life, her first thought was of the grave. The bag of hair was in the kitchen. It lay on the table and she picked it up and held it to the light from the window. It was almost devoid of colour, certainly not the dark cap that had so delighted them, but she didn't see that as a problem. It was old and anyway there was nothing more she could do. When Terry rang, she would arrange for him to collect it and then await the outcome.

Chapter 26

He didn't look at it. When Terry came to collect what he referred to as 'the lock of hair', she had put the plastic bag into a small brown envelope. She handed it to him and he made no attempt to open it.

"How are you, Lily?"

"I'm alright, thank you."

In truth, she was feeling stronger. In the two days since she had called him, her spirits had strengthened. She had looked forward to seeing Terry again, the prospect cheered her. She was clearer now about what she was doing. The end might still be hidden in mist, but each step forward gave her strength. Revenge. She didn't shy from the word.

They were sitting in the living room. He waved the envelope in the air. "I appreciate this. I can only imagine how hard it must be for you and I'm very grateful."

He must never know how hard it had been. She wanted to let him know that she wasn't an old fogey with no understanding of technology. "I looked it up, what they need. I think that will do."

"Thank you."

"Will you let me know? Please, will you keep me informed about what happens?"

"Of course I will. It won't be fast. It's not just a simple test and it could take a few weeks. I've been researching. I know where I'm going to send it. I'm waiting for a kit from them, to get a sample from *him*." As Terry spoke he rose from the settee and crossed the small space between them. Lily was astounded when he bent to kiss her cheek. "I'll tell you everything that's going on. I'm determined now, with all of this, I am determined that he's going to pay, for this at least. I'll come again, maybe next week if that's alright? See how you are, let you know what's happening."

"Oh, yes please. That would be wonderful. Thank you."

"Hey, I meant what I said. I'm the one who's grateful and after all you've been through, you deserve to be kept in the picture. Then, when it's all over, we'll take the ashes." He nodded towards the china cabinet. "We'll bury them, but only if you still want to."

And the brief sunshine went out of her world, because of course he didn't know.

"If it's proved that he is Peter's father, what will you do?"

He had regained his seat on the settee and before he answered, Terry took a moment, collecting his thoughts, or maybe deciding how best to explain his plan.

"So, the first thing is to get the tests done. It all hinges on them really. I could go to the authorities even before that, and tell them about what he did to me, but that feels a bit feeble. After all this time, what would be the point anyway?"

"I thought you wanted to expose him?"

"Yes, I do. But it's going to be so much better to have solid proof. Scientific evidence of what he did with his own daughter, as well as benefitting by selling the baby instead of doing the right thing, and taking responsibility."

This was the first time he had named the crime so very clearly. As he did she saw him clench his fists, and a nerve in his jaw jumped under the skin.

"Well, right..." He paused. "I'll have powerful ammunition to expose him. Most of these cases, the ones that you see on the news, the victims have been outsiders, haven't they? Pupils or – oh, I don't know, choir boys, you know what I mean, and it's hearsay and just victims trying to convince people. I couldn't face that. All the doubt that there always is, but with this..." He held up the envelope. "It's irrefutable, isn't it? Everyone knows that this goes on in families, uncles, cousins, and I suppose aunts as well sometimes, and yes, fathers. I'm not a crusader. I wish I was, I wish I was that brave, but, to be honest, I just think that I want to shame him. This is about me and him.

"I know some people will probably say I've only done it for the money, but I don't need to. I have all I need now, okay I don't *own* it, but I will in time. But it would be good to see it taken away from him when they throw him in jail. Mainly, I just want to let people know and for me to feel that he didn't get away scot-free. When I was younger I wished him dead, over and over. I would pretend, when I woke up in the morning, I would pretend that he was lying there in the next room dead. I still do sometimes. But maybe it'll be enough for me to be able to take everything away from him.

"All these years of pretending that we were ordinary. It's there every day, you know? No matter how hard you try to push it away. Well perhaps it'll be enough to let people know that he is anything but normal."

"Do you think there was ever anyone else?"

"Oh shit, I have thought about that so much. I've tried to remember, you know, if there were kids around the house when I was younger. He was never in charge of any kids but..."

"Yes?" Lily urged him on.

"I think it's possible. He was a landlord. He had plenty of flats and he used to do the rounds, collecting rents. He did it himself back in those days. Before it was all done by direct debit and standing order. There were rent books and he used to go and collect cash. Sometimes he would take me with him."

Lily nodded, and listened quietly.

He carried on, "Mostly I went in with him, to the houses, the flats. He used to say he was training me. Sometimes I was plonked in front of the television while he had a 'talk' with the woman who was there, usually upstairs or in the front rooms. But, every so often, he would make me wait in the car. Sometimes we'd have other blokes with us, his friends, and I was told not to talk to them, keep my mouth shut. I would sit in the back seat and there was a feeling about it all that used to scare me. Then they'd go into places, houses mostly but sometimes shops or workshops. He'd give me some sweets, put the radio on." Terry shook his head. "I didn't ask questions, but now – well I just wonder and I hate the conclusions I come to. When you're in that sort of situation you just count your blessings when nothing happens to you. The whole thing is hideous."

Again, Lily nodded her understanding. She spoke low and quiet, "So, if there were other women, children maybe, do you think you'd get them to come forward?"

"I don't know. It's possible, isn't it?"

"It's going to ruin your family."

"There is no family left. There was only ever the four of us. It doesn't matter, there's nothing left to ruin. Well nothing but him and that's the idea. Before you came, showing me that receipt and telling me about what had happened to my mum's other baby, to my brother, well I had pretty much given up. I thought I'd just wait until the old swine gave up and died. I decided that I could just wait and then enjoy spending his money. Whatever is left when the nursing home is paid for. He's in the lap of luxury even now and it's not on, not any more. Now, though, when I think of what he put her through, and me – and I don't know, maybe there are others – now, I think I want it all to come out."

"All of it?"

"Yes, all of it, it's sort of the next best thing to seeing him dead and gone. Maybe it's even better than that. I have thought about it, yes. It's going to have an effect on you, isn't it? I have been worried about it. I need to put some ideas to you. Are you well enough?"

She realised that she had frightened him with the attack in the pub, it made him seem so very sweet, vulnerable. "Yes, I'm alright. I'm feeling better these last few days." And she was, sometimes she forgot how ill she was and planned for a future, one that was free of the guilt, one where she had made some sort of recompense. It was novel and very pleasant.

"Good. Yes, that's great. So, I'll tell you what I have thought and you can take some time, consider the idea, and then let me know what you feel. I don't want to cause you trouble, you didn't do anything wrong, not you personally."

She couldn't answer him, she turned away and took the mugs into the kitchen. She looked from where she stood by the sink and stared at the cellar door. If he knew, would he still think she had done no wrong?

Chapter 27

When Lily went back into the living room, Terry was looking out of the window, his back to the room. He obviously didn't know she was there and she watched him, quietly. His hands were clenched behind him and his head bowed. She heard him sniff, he pushed a hand into his jeans pocket to take out his handkerchief, and as he wiped at his eyes she was overwhelmed with tenderness.

She turned and crept back into the hall and stamped her feet on the carpet. By the time she came through the door a second time, he had turned, and was stepping back towards the settee.

"So, your plan?" She smiled at him as she spoke. Her arms ached to hug him. She wanted to ease his hurt. All the years of longing for the baby in the basement were concentrated in this room. All the nurturing instincts that had been subdued and denied were flooding through her, and she felt strange, light-headed.

He was serious as he answered her. "If I'm to use the fact that Clive sold his own baby then, obviously, I have to be able to say who bought him, where he went. You do see that, don't you?"

"Yes, of course."

"But I don't want to make you suffer any more than you have done. You've told me that it was Charlotte who started it, and that you didn't know anything about it. I believe you. I think that you would have made a good mother for him, if he'd lived. I don't know about her obviously, but you... Yes, I think you would have been a good mum, and I think it's horrible that you weren't given the chance. So, why don't we simply leave you out of it?"

"I don't see what you mean. I don't see how we can do that. I was here, I held him."

"I know, but it was such a short time. From what you said nobody saw him. You didn't take him out?"

Lily shook her head.

"So, is it possible to pretend you didn't know until she died and you were given those things? Is it possible that she could have had him and not told you? We could make up some story about the urn, the cremation, just make out that you didn't know any of it and you're as shocked as anyone."

She'd been a coward long enough, she wasn't doing that any more.

"No, we lived together. We were nearly always together, up until then, until his death came between us."

"You said she had an affair."

"Yes, but it was a sordid little incident. A few afternoons sneaking away with someone who was young and interesting. I don't think she ever really intended to leave me." Lily paused. "I don't think she did but... Oh, none of that matters any more, does it? The point is, nobody would believe she could bring a baby home and I wouldn't know."

She thought for a minute before continuing. "Though I haven't got many of our friends from back then, there are enough to raise doubt. If they become aware of it all, and they surely must, they'll be shaking their heads and having their say." She drew in a deep breath. "Look, Terry, I think that anything that will weaken your case, anything that will give people something to point at and say *well, that's not true*, has to be discounted. Let's just go forward and see what happens. I'm old Terry, I'm old and spent and tired, and if the last thing I can do is to help you find some sort of peace then, well it might make up for... It might make up for what we did."

Terry took out his handkerchief again and blew his nose. "Thank you. Thank you, Lily. It's true, what I said, you would have made a wonderful mother."

* * *

He had gone and Lily felt exhausted, mentally and physically, but her spirits had lifted. The cloud of depression that had become so much part of her every day had been driven back. What had been a background dread, had become a real possibility, and oddly, it was easier to handle. Her mind was alive with plans.

She went downstairs and spoke to the baby in the grave. "Well, little man. People are going to know about you. Not everything, I'm sorry, not all of it. I will have to keep this little secret, won't I? But they will know you *were*, they'll know your name. We're moving forward. It's all going to work out."

She heard knocking upstairs and went to answer the door to Sandra. Her neighbour carried a plate with a cloth over it. She held it forward. "I won't come in, I'm expecting Roger, but I made a casserole, chicken. Will you have some?" The aroma, drifting from under the cover made Lily's mouth water, suddenly, she felt ravenous.

"Thank you. Thank you very much. I really do appreciate your kindness." She took the plate.

Sandra beamed at her. "You're looking better. How are you feeling?"

"Yes, better, thank you."

"I saw your visitor leaving. Is that Charlotte's nephew, the one you told me about?"

"No, he's just a friend. A dear friend."

"Well, he's done you good, coming here. It's nice to see you so much brighter."

Lily sat at the kitchen table. She ate the casserole, which was delicious, and then she went upstairs and crawled under the covers. She felt herself falling into a dark, warm space and she let herself go. She slept until morning, her dreams were vivid but they were kind – sunshine and happiness.

Chapter 28

She filled the days with sorting and cleaning, and she waited.

In the quiet house, several times she picked up her phone, opened the contacts list and looked at his name. She knew that there was no point calling him. He had told her that he had to wait for the DNA kit, to take a sample from his grandfather.

She did some more research online, but it wasn't possible to get a clear idea of how long it would take for the result to be sent to him. The calibre of the lab he had chosen, the samples he had from his mother's belongings – there was so much information that she wasn't a party to.

Every evening, she took a new candle down into the cellar. She carried a folding chair one day and placed it in the corner near to the grave.

Sometimes she would talk, but often sat in silence, watched the flame, and let her mind wander. She remembered the years with Charlotte Mary. The ups and downs, and though there was much to regret, there had been good times too and she found herself smiling at those memories.

She recalled the awful days when Peter had died, the terrible arguments about what they should do and the dreadful decision that they came to. She had always believed it was wrong and knew it had blighted the rest of her existence. Charlotte Mary seemed to have shrugged it off, but now, there was this legacy of the tiny plastic bracelet and the clue to his name and origin. How sad, she had believed they knew each other so very well and it hadn't been true. She wondered what other options they could have chosen and how much difference it would have made. Too late, all too late.

Sitting in the gloom, she remembered her own childhood, her mother and father. Maybe, she thought, all this introspection was just her life moving towards the end. She knew that it was. The pain came often, the breathlessness and a feeling of exhaustion. Perhaps this was nature's way of cleaning and tidying, preparing the way. She should be glad of it, should find comfort in the fact that there had been some warning of how little time there was left.

Charlotte Mary had fought it, every day had been a battle, and in the end, she had been war-weary and demented. As she had sat beside the storm-tossed bed, Lily had wondered whether it would not have been kinder to end it for her. Surely there was a way, a kind way to stop the struggle. A pillow placed gently while she slept. How long would it take? Would she have the courage? She had picked up one of the cushions from the small sofa and gripped it tight in her hands. She had moved to stand at the head of the bed, but then her resolve had faltered and, throwing the thing aside, she had been ashamed. Not because she had almost done it, but because in the end she hadn't. It wasn't right to watch this suffering and not be able to ease the torment.

That wasn't the way that Lily wanted it to be, and she collected more pills. She was stockpiling them, storing them away in the bathroom cabinet, and when she was ready, they would be waiting. She was glad now that she hadn't done it on that other dreadful day. She blessed whatever instinct had stayed her hand. She wanted to see this thing through, to find the truth about the baby and see Terry have justice. This alone was enough to give her the strength to keep going.

In the china cabinet was another unfinished task. She should fix that. Terry no longer needed ashes for the DNA testing, now he had something much better. She could dispose of them. Where would she choose? The Solent? No. Charlotte Mary had never been a beach person. Portsdown Hill? Above the town. No, it wasn't right. Although Southsea had been their home for decades it wasn't where they were from. Charlotte Mary had been born abroad, the Far East, and had travelled, far and often. Though there had been stories, there was nowhere that she had said felt like home. Nowhere that she had been called back to.

When the answer came to her, Lily was surprised that it had taken so long. School had been the only place they had talked of often. The people, the occurrences, the daily trials and triumphs. That was where their happiness had been most untrammelled. Their closeness and their obvious kicking over the traces, their unhidden relationship, had made them special, infamous in a rather delicious way that they had never experienced again. Charlotte Mary had revelled in it. Yes, when the time came she would take what was left of her and leave her in the quad. There was a small area of shrubbery, a tiny fountain. That was where she would go.

But then, Terry had wanted something of Peter to bury with his mother, something to take to a grave. The thought lurked on the sidelines, but she pushed it aside, struggled with it, knew that it would be her final undoing. But it would not be denied. She would need to be brave and accept that he would turn against her, so it would be a final act. Then she would be able to die, calm and at peace.

Maybe, if she achieved something even better than she had first planned, more than just giving Peter back to his mother and to his brother, maybe that would be enough.

She would wait until the proper time and then would make it all right. Better than right, she would do a good thing and it felt like the first really good thing that she had done for many years.

On Wednesday, Terry called. "I was going to try and come and see you, Lily, but I won't be able to make it this week after all. I just wanted to let you know, I have the kit now and tomorrow I am going to see Clive. I'm going to get the sample from him and then I will send it all away."

It was a disappointment, she wanted to see him again, but also, she had hoped that they would be further along with it than they were. When she had considered it, she had imagined the laboratory working on the samples, doing whatever it was they did to access the magic of DNA.

"Oh, that's fine. Terry, do you have any idea when you might come?" She didn't want to drive him away with her neediness, but hadn't been able to hold her tongue. "Just so that I can be sure to be here," she said.

"Yes, Monday. I'll come on Monday. Maybe we could go out to lunch. Would you be able to do that, do you think? Have you time?"

"That would be lovely." She smiled, a true and genuine smile that reached her eyes.

Chapter 29

It had been a long time since Lily had gone out to eat. Charlotte Mary refused to be seen in public after she lost her hair.

She would book a table, but nowhere too busy. Eventually she decided on a small place, a Victorian villa, converted and recently refurbished. She looked at the reviews online and it seemed to promise good food, good service, and would not be buzzing with children and thumping music. She booked a table and sorted a clean skirt and sweater from the dowdy depths of her wardrobe.

Terry was late. There wasn't time for conversation, and they scuttled from the house minutes after he arrived. He wondered if they should drive. Lily told him that, no, she would be fine provided they didn't walk too quickly.

The restaurant was clean and warm, the food was good, and they shared a half-bottle of wine. Lily enjoyed herself more than she had for an age. They discussed the weather, the traffic, politics, in a superficial way, and she relaxed and enjoyed his company. It was like coming back to life.

Once they were back at her home she made coffee, not the instant sort that they had drunk before, but freshly ground beans she had bought in preparation.

She fussed with the pot and cups, gave him a chance to broach the subject that filled the air between them. In the end, it fell to Lily to make the first move. "How is it going Terry, with the tests?"

He nodded, relieved. "Okay, I went to the nursing home. Clive was having a good day as it happened. I had some business things to discuss. I had to wait until he was asleep. The lab sent me a thing like a cotton bud, and it had to go into his mouth, rubbed on his cheek. I had no way to ask him to do that. I just couldn't come up with any sort of reason. Anyway, when he was asleep, snoring his head off actually, I was able to do it fairly easily. He has drugs of course and once he's out of it, well, he is completely out of it. I reckon you could do just about anything with him then. I cut a couple of his fingernails as well. They gave me options so I thought I'd do both. I sent it all away and now I'm just waiting. I've asked for paternal and maternal testing. I sent them the hair, Peter's hair. It was still in the bag that you put it in. I thought that was best. I suppose it was because it was so old, but it didn't really look like the pictures on the instruction leaflets. The ends were odd, clumpy somehow."

Lily delivered the answer that she had prepared on the day that she gave him the sample. "I didn't do it. It was Charlotte, after he died. She just wanted to keep it. I hope it will be alright."

He shrugged. "If it's not I suppose they'll come back to me and then, well, we've always got the ashes. Did you have much of a funeral for him? I don't suppose you could, under the circumstances. Poor little thing, not even that."

She shook her head and looked away. She didn't want to lie to him anymore.

After a minute, he continued, "I sent them Mum's old toothbrush, and her hairbrush. I told them she was dead. I've spoken to them, told them the baby and the mother are both dead. To be honest they didn't ask that many questions. They charge a small fortune, and you have to pay up front, so I think mainly they just want your money. Anyway, that's what I've done." He stopped and laughed quietly. "A bit disgusting that Mum's stuff was still in the cupboard, but she had her own bathroom and I've sort of left it alone. Her rooms are closed up. I don't go in there much at all. It's all a bit pathetic really – miserable. He could have done much better for her, but she never asked him for much."

"Was he violent with her?"

"Huh, what you mean apart from the fact that he made her have sex with him? Sorry, sorry that was uncalled for. If you mean did he hit her? Well, not as far as I know. Not that I ever saw. But she feared him, she tried to keep out of his way. I would get mad with her, when I was younger. I didn't understand. He shouted a lot and I wanted her to stand up for us, she never did. I needed her to do it because of what he was doing to me. But I couldn't tell her and yet, I wanted her to protect me. Well, she couldn't, could she? My gran used to ignore him, they hardly spoke. I thought everyone's family was like that, until later, when I was more independent and had friends that I visited. Once I was older, bigger than him, I used to ask him for money, clothes, stuff like that. He didn't argue with me anymore then. He started to treat me better. It was too late though, far too late. No matter what he did, he couldn't make up for the past."

"Terry, did you never think about reporting him, or at least facing him with it? What he'd done to you?"

"No. Once it was over, when I was about thirteen, he backed off. I was relieved. Every week when he didn't…" He shrugged, unable to say out loud what had been done. He tried again, "Every week that went by, when I'd been left alone, was a bonus. But it was a long time before I could believe that it was over. I thought that if I faced him with it, it might all start again. Like poking at a wasp's nest. Then, when I was big enough to be sure that I could stop him, I didn't need to mention it, not outright. Once I wasn't a kid anymore he tried to win me over, gave me things, brought me into the business but, no, we didn't talk about it. Of course, I didn't know the whole story about Mum. I just thought he was mean to her, a bully. If I'd known, If I'd had any idea about how bad it all was, things would have been very different. Anyway, she was ill when she told me. She knew she was dying. He'd had the stroke, I suppose she waited until she felt safe."

He squeezed at his eyes with his fingertips, coughed. "Poor Mum, she never grew too big for him, did she? Anyway, she told me about the abuse. But then, much later when she told me she'd had a baby that had been adopted, I never put two and two together. I was still pretty young and you don't want to hear things like that, about your mum I mean. She didn't tell me that much, I suppose it was just too painful for her to go into all the details. That would have been the time for me to confess, to tell her about me. But I couldn't give her even more pain, and it wouldn't have changed things.

"He went straight to the nursing home from the hospital. Then, not long afterwards, Mum died. He and I just slipped into the sort of relationship that we have now. I see him about once a month, he signs papers, leases and suchlike and that's it."

"So, it's still his business?"

Terry nodded. "I did try at one stage to take control, have him sign over a power of attorney, but it went nowhere. He's got a solicitor who's worked for him as long as I can remember and he was obstructive. Accused me of money-grabbing and what have you. It just didn't seem worth struggling with to be honest. I was enjoying my life, so it all just drifted along. On my own, no more worries."

"No girlfriend then? Or boyfriend?"

"No, I've had a couple of relationships, girls." He grinned at her, a fleeting brightness. "But they never went anywhere."

For a minute, there was silence, not comfortable but stuffy with things not said, questions unasked. Lily was afraid of driving him away, of being too inquisitive. She spoke first though, "What's the next step then? I mean once you have the results and if they are what we think. If he is Peter's father, exactly what will you do?"

"I'll go and face him with it. I'll tell him what I know, show him the receipt, the results from the lab, and let him know that I'm going to the police. I'll tell him that I'm reporting what he did to me for years, me and Mum. If I have the proof, even if he denies it, it doesn't alter the fact that he forced me to do the things he did, and that he had sex with his own daughter. I just want to see his face. I want to see his fear." He was wringing his hands now.

Lily leaned and stilled them by briefly laying her own on top of them. "Does it scare you, Terry?"

"Yes, a bit. After all this time. But it's so that I can live with myself. I'll do it. It's scares me, yes, but I'll do it."

"Is there anything I can do? Anything at all that I can do to help?"

He didn't answer for a long time and Lily thought she had overstepped the mark, pushed too much. But eventually, he rubbed his hands together and spoke quietly, "Well, maybe there is something. Would you come with me?"

She whispered, "To the nursing home?"

"Yes. You know about it already, you're the only person who does. Would you come with me if the results are what we expect?"

She didn't hesitate. It was exactly what she had wanted. "Yes. I will. I will come with you."

Chapter 30

Two weeks passed. Lily called the solicitor and made an appointment to update her will. It had to be done now that she owned everything. She had intended to leave it all to Charlotte Mary's nephew, but now, with this new young man in her life, she was rethinking – was there something for Terry? Something to ensure that in the years to come he wouldn't forget her. But then she realised that there was no need. He wouldn't forget her. When he knew the whole truth, she didn't think he would ever forget her and it didn't appear that he needed her money.

The night before the appointment with Mr Barnstable, she sat at the desk and spent a long time with the letter. It had to be clear, the *why* of it all. No excuses, just reasons, simple and concise. Eventually she was happy with it. She sealed the envelope and wrote Terry's name on the front. With a bit of luck there would be time to speak to him in person but, just in case, she now had a safety net.

Another task accomplished. Still the days dragged on. With failing strength and the narrowing of her world, it was difficult to fill them. She visited the neighbours, more to make the time pass more quickly than from any real sense of friendship. All the while that Sandra chattered on, about the garden, the church, the weather, Lily's thoughts were in Bath, or in the basement, or in contemplation of the darkness to come.

Eventually the call came. "Lily, it's me, Terry. I've got the results. Shall I come to your home or do you want me to tell you now?"

She bit back her impatience. He had obviously realised that she might want to savour this. It was too big to pass in a moment on the phone, so he had offered the choice. "Please, will you come, Terry?"

"This afternoon?"

"Yes. Please."

When the phone call was finished, she went into the cellar. "It's time, Peter. It's time. This is the last stretch." She felt too excited to sit still.

She had a shower, changed her clothes, and tidied the rooms. The morning crawled by. Her heart pounded and she took some of the calming tablets, but only half the dose. It would be no good if she was drowsy and befuddled.

At last there was the rattle of the gate. Terry passed in front of the bay without glancing up, and then was lost from sight as he entered the porch. She was stepping over a threshold, she must hold her nerve now. The next few minutes would decide how her end would come, maybe even where she would be. The thought both terrified and thrilled her.

* * *

There was no pretence that this was a pleasant social visit. It was business and hard business at that. Terry carried a brown envelope. Lily ushered him into the dining room where there was room for them to sit together at the large table. Space for the sheets of paper.

He slapped the documents onto the shining wood and slid them towards her. His face gave nothing away. 'Stony', that was the way she would have described it.

"You've read it?"

"I have. There's quite a lot of technical stuff. I hadn't really expected that. When you see it on the television they show you one piece of paper. I think it's mostly to make you feel that you got value for money. As it turns out there is one that has the conclusion on. I put it on the top, but if you want to read the other stuff, it's fine."

Lily shook her head, she didn't expect to understand, and it wouldn't change anything. She tipped the envelope, slid her hand inside to pull out the sheaf of printed sheets. She closed her eyes for a moment. Terry was quiet beside her. How had it been for him? Had he torn it open with desperate fingers or made the moment last as she was doing? Later they could talk about all of that.

The text was clear. It was easy to understand. Her hands began to shake as she read the conclusion over twice, and then looked at him. His face was still a blank.

Lily murmured into the quiet room, "So..."

"Yes. I know they always have to put it in those terms, they can never say absolutely, covering their backsides, but there we have it. Clive, my grandfather, is Peter's father, and my mum was his mum, Peter's mum."

His voice deserted him, neither of them knew what to say. How very odd it was. They had known this, both of them. They had never really had any doubt, and now on this quiet afternoon they were overwhelmed with emotion because they had been right.

Terry coughed. "There's more, Lily. There's something else I have to tell you." He was ashen, all the colour had drained from his face. The pink in his cheeks, the result of his walk from the seafront, was obliterated.

"More?"

"The lab has done another test."

Lily's heart thundered. He had realised that the sample she had given him was newly harvested, from a long-dead child. He had mentioned the strange appearance of it. Maybe the lab had been in contact about it. She flopped onto the dining chair.

"I hadn't ever thought of this, Lily. I was probably being stupid. But with everything, well, I should have seen." He closed his eyes, drew in a breath.

Chapter 31

Lily couldn't look at him, she couldn't bear to see the disgust in his face, the flicker of hate maybe, in his eyes. Already her mind was forming excuses, reasons, more lies. She forced herself to concentrate, to listen to his words.

He was speaking quietly, his eyes fixed on their hands clasped together on the table top. "I imagine that you might have already thought of this, Lily, and I wonder why you never suggested it, but then, you're kind, so…"

His words were not making sense, 'kind' was not how she saw herself. How could he think her anything but evil? She'd had his brother buried without marker or recognition in the dark sadness of her basement. She had let him die to protect herself, that was how she had cared for a helpless child, and he thought her kind!

"Anyway, I sent them my finger nails." He couldn't go on. When Lily looked up she saw despair in his face, the sadness of betrayal.

"I always believed her. Why wouldn't I? She was my mum. I never imagined anything other than I was told. When you came to me with this stuff, at first it didn't even occur to me, then as time went on I didn't have a lot of choice. I wasn't sure right up to when I sent the stuff off."

He struggled for control. "In the end, though, I knew I had no other option." He pushed his hand into the pocket of his leather jacket. He placed another piece of paper on the table. It was face down, and as Lily turned it over and began to read, Terry stood abruptly and stormed across the room to stare out of the window into the back garden.

"Oh, Terry." Lily laid the paper aside and went to stand beside him. She took his hand and turned him towards her. "Terry, I hadn't thought of this. You told me your history and I never questioned it. Terry, this, this…" She pointed towards the table. "This doesn't matter, it doesn't make you anything other than you have always been."

"Doesn't make any difference! Lily, I don't even know if there's a name for what I am. A bastard, yes, but I was always that, that didn't matter, it's true. But my grandfather's bastard, with my mum, his own daughter. What the hell does that make me? I don't even know if there is a name for what we are to each other." He snatched his hand away and fled from the room. She saw him moments later, out in her garden, pacing back and forth, kicking at the lawn edging.

Lily had thought that she started down this road with good intentions. She had wanted to ease her conscience before she died. She had wanted to make sure Peter would not be forgotten, and she had intended only to let the other woman know what had happened to her baby. She had imagined tears of gratitude, a plan to lay the child somewhere better. She had hoped for absolution. It had gone so badly wrong that, not only was she deeper in the mire of deception, but she had ruined another life. Anger built as she watched through the window – what evil there was in the world, and this was evil unpunished. It mustn't stand, but for now, she wasn't yet sure of what could be done, but if it was her last act on earth she would do whatever she could to avenge the two sons of Clive Robertson.

She didn't know what she could say to Terry, how to make amends for the desolation she had seen on his face. She heard him walk back into the kitchen, through the hall, and then he appeared in the doorway.

"I don't know what to do next, Lily. I don't know which way to turn now. I should never have asked them to check my DNA. I was stupid and now I can't undo any of it."

"If you hadn't done that, your intention was to face him with what he'd done. Can you not carry on with that?"

"Carry on, carry on…!" He had raised his voice and when Lily flinched he held up a hand. "Sorry, I don't mean to take it out on you. It's just that I can't even bear the thought of seeing him right now. Why is it that people like him get to live, Lily, and yet people like my mum have their lives ruined, and that poor little sod, my brother, didn't even get a chance to grow up?"

"I understand. I think I understand anyway. But there is another way to look at this."

"Another way. No, it's there. It's there in front of you on the table. There are no other ways. It's there in black and white, proven by science. He is my bloody father." He sat down heavily on the dining chair and Lily reached for him, but he didn't take her hand.

"Terry, he always knew this. He knew he was your father. He must have done, but he doesn't know that you have had these tests done. So, you can just carry on, you could do what you intended. Go to the police, if you want to. Report his abuse. Or, you don't need to tell anyone else about this. You can destroy that piece of paper and never refer to it again."

He shook his head before responding, "It doesn't change it though, does it? Denying something doesn't make it untrue."

Of course, she had no answer for him because so much of her life had been about learning to live with exactly that.

"Calm down, just calm down. I'll pour a drink. We'll talk. I am sorry, I truly am, but Terry…"

He turned to her. Waited.

"Terry, don't let it take your future. Let me help you to face him. If you must do that and maybe when you do, things will become clearer. You don't have to speak about this to anyone else. Take your time. Stay with me, tonight. Stay here. Sleep here, and then tomorrow we'll go together to Bath. We'll go and see him."

She wasn't ready, but events had overtaken her and really, it didn't matter. She wanted more than anything in the world to ease Terry's pain, and she believed she knew how to do it. She had already played it out in her mind. Not the fine details, that wasn't possible yet, but the intention.

"No, I need to go back. I have things to do. Thank you, but no."

"Alright then, but I'll come tomorrow, or the day after, whenever you say, and I'll go with you."

"Okay. Yes, okay. Tomorrow. Shall I come for you?"

"No, it's an easy journey, I'll be fine."

And so the die was cast.

He didn't stay much longer. He couldn't settle. He needed to be moving, and she imagined it had been like that ever since he had read the test results. She let him go, there were things that she must do herself. She logged onto the computer and ordered a ticket for the train. Organised the rest of it.

She walked around the house. Remembering, taking it all in, firming up the memories. Then of course she went down into the basement. She told Peter her plans and sat for a while with him.

Although things were moving quickly, it didn't matter. She was glad in many ways. It would all be over sooner, and that was good. She felt strong and she felt needed.

Chapter 32

Lily walked out of the station and over the Halfpenny Bridge. There was a grey heron fishing in the pond beside the lock. Crowds pushed past her, they didn't see her, their busy lives rendered her invisible. She walked painfully onwards.

Later, when she had taken care of her tasks, she called Terry, and the phone went to his answering service. "Hello, it's Lily. I'm in Bath. I can meet you in town if you like. I'll go and find somewhere to have a cup of coffee. Just let me know when you're ready."

She went back to the place that she had used the first time. The quiet little tea shop. There was a band of pain around her chest; she was gasping for breath and her finger ends tingled. She sent up a silent prayer, not for ease, but only that she wouldn't have to go on much longer. Just a little while, she needed a short while. She needed to stay strong.

She felt a frisson of fear. Charlotte Mary's death had been difficult. The cries and struggle agonising to witness. She wouldn't allow that to happen to her. She would manage it. All through her life she had been carried by the flow of events, that one final act would be hers to orchestrate and control. She had brought the pills with her, just in case she didn't have the strength for the journey home. She needed to get back if it was possible, but had what people these days referred to as a Plan B.

She had placed her phone on the table and when it began to vibrate she snatched it up. It was him. "Terry. Hello. Did you hear my message?"

"Yes. Sorry, I was driving. So, you're here early."

"Yes, but don't worry. I can wait until you're ready. Are you alright, about this, I mean?"

"Well, let's say I won't be any more alright if I put it off. So, we might as well get it done."

"Do you want to talk about it?" She detected hesitation and wanted to give him the chance to back out, though that would be a complication.

"No. I just want to get on and scare the shit out of the old swine. Sorry for the language."

She laughed. "Oh, that's alright. Charlotte Mary used to swear like a docker. I never had her knack, but I used to enjoy the look on people's faces when she did it."

"You must miss her terribly."

She had no answer. She missed something, surely. She missed the presence of someone in her life, because there had always been someone. She missed the quiet comfort of a companion to eat a meal with, and she missed the reassurance of having someone there when the pain was so bad that she was convinced she was about to die alone. There were times when she was beset by the idea that no-one would find her for days, and she would be sprawled, undignified on the carpet. But she wasn't sure that she missed Charlotte Mary. She had been absent for longer than she had been dead, and even before that, they had become little more than a habit to each other, or perhaps a mutual crutch as the days shortened and the regrets were greater than the joy.

She had lost herself to the musing and was dragged back by his voice.

"Hello, hello. Lily, can you hear me?"

"Yes, sorry. It's a bit noisy. Where shall I meet you?"

"Can you make your way to St Michael's Church? Do you know where that is?"

"Yes, I think I can remember."

"I can be there in about ten minutes. Oh, I just thought, you don't know my car. It's a black VW, a Golf."

By the time the car pulled into the kerb and she saw Terry waving through the windscreen it had started to rain. She had forgotten her umbrella and knew that her hair would have frizzed with damp. She wasn't vain, but in her mind was the impression she had been hoping to give, and a bedraggled old woman in a damp coat hadn't been the plan. No matter, she would work with what she was given.

Terry didn't speak, he was stiff and pale with tension. His mood was catching and they drove in silence, out of the city and up into the countryside.

The nursing home was set in acres of lawns and trees, there was a lake and flower borders. As they walked under the stone portico and stepped inside the hall there was no smell of age and decay, which is what Lily had expected. Instead there was the scent of flowers, the clean smell of furniture polish, and the woman seated behind a reception desk wore a neat suit. The only indications that it was anything other than a smart hotel were the nurses walking with quiet purpose. There was a discrete notice which suggested visiting times and a schedule for when the doors would be locked, and callers would need to use the side entrance.

The staff wore what Lily had always thought were *proper* uniforms: dark dresses with neat white collars and black tights.

"It's very nice, Terry."

"Yes. It should be, it costs an arm and a leg."

The receptionist had approached them, her hand extended. "Good afternoon, Mr Robertson. It's nice to see you again."

"Hello Rachel. How is my grandfather?"

"He's having a good day. We had to have the doctor look at him yesterday, his blood pressure is a little troublesome at times. It's a worry, but we are keeping an eye on it. The physiotherapist has put him on a different schedule and his mobility is improving. He may be well enough to have a trip away from The Grange in another week or two. Always providing he is stable of course."

"Right. Well, that's good."

Lily saw from the woman's reaction that she had expected more delight, more interest from Terry. He was struggling, she knew that, and he was subdued.

There was a moment of awkward silence. She clutched at her chest, suddenly, dramatically. Terry and the receptionist turned to her as she gave a groan. "Oh Terry, I'm sorry. I need to sit down. I'm sorry."

They reached for her and helped her to a seat. They fussed. The receptionist suggested they call one of the nurses.

"No, no, really. Just give me a moment. I'll be fine. Perhaps a drink of water?"

"Oh, of course." The young woman ran through the door at one side of the hallway. She returned with a glass of water and was accompanied by a nurse who carried a case, or a bag, something medical and rather frightening.

Lily took out the spray, used it, and laid her head against the chair back. She closed her eyes. It was difficult for her to draw attention to herself in this way. Now that she had, however, she was confident that they would remember her.

Chapter 33

Terry had suggested that they come back another day when Lily might be feeling better. She saw in his face something of a frightened child, trying to be brave, but detecting one small chance of escape. This was her own first scary step along a frightening road, there was a chance still to pull back, but the days of cowardice were over.

"I'm fine. These attacks come often. They catch me unprepared sometimes, but the medicine works."

"Is there nothing they can do?"

They were still in the hallway, he was bending close to her. The nurse and receptionist had moved away, but watched, ready to step in should they be needed. She smiled at them and lifted a hand, reassuring.

"There are some things they have suggested," she answered Terry honestly, but didn't tell him that she had made the decision to let the disease have its way. "I don't really feel up to it at the moment. We'll see what happens." She patted his hand and then laid hers onto his arm and he helped her to her feet. They walked together up the sweeping staircase.

* * *

Terry didn't knock on the heavy wooden door but neither did he burst in. He pushed it slightly open and stood to one side, so that he could look inside without exposing the interior to the corridor. He nodded, and pushed it further open.

It was a bright, spacious room. Pale walls, heavy curtains, and though the bed was a traditional hospital one, the rest of the furniture was beautiful old wood or smart upholstery. At first, she couldn't see anyone, but the chair, pulled into the curve of a bay window, was occupied. Terry walked over to stand before the old man. He was propped up with pillows and a blanket had been draped over his thin knees.

Lily had tried to imagine what Clive Robertson might look like. She was still searching for an image of Peter, of what he would have become. This skinny, sallow-faced person, his sparse hair combed neatly, his face cleanly shaven, came nowhere near to what she hoped for. How could this frail creature have held such sway over his family, how could he have bullied his wife, his daughter, and his grandson in the way that she had been led to believe. Terry wasn't a big man, but he was no weakling either. His body was wiry, but he was muscular and moved with the confidence of health and youth. But then, for most of it he had been a child, a frightened, confused little boy. Wasn't it true that bullies weren't always the biggest, they were just the ones who knew how to manipulate, and who didn't let things like conscience and humanity stop them taking whatever they wanted, however they wanted.

As if he had read her thoughts, Terry moved to the table beside the bed and picked up a trifold picture frame.

"When he first came, they asked me to bring something like this." He held it out to her. "They said it helped to motivate patients. Huh."

He pointed. "That's their wedding day, him and Granny. That's my mum and me, later, when I was at school."

She saw that years and illness had reduced what had been a tall, well-built, barrel-chested individual to the thin, old man who was now waking from the doze he had been in when they first arrived. The third image was Clive Robertson, standing alone in a grand hall, in evening dress, but there was no woman at his side in a glamorous gown. No wife leaned proudly on his arm. But he looked confident, sure of himself.

Terry stood beside her looking down at the images. "Happy families. Bloody hell, what a joke. He married my gran because her family had property. Once she inherited, he had her sign the management of it over to him, all for the best, all so that she wouldn't have to worry about things like that, once she became a mother.

"Then my mum, when she was young, she couldn't have friends over, she couldn't go on school trips, she couldn't go and stay with other people. He would say that Gran needed her, that it wasn't right that she wanted to be away from the family. I think he used to hit my gran. I know I said he didn't hit Mum but I was a kid, what did I know? I never saw it, but with Granny there must have been a reason, mustn't there? There was something he did to reduce her to the way she was, she just shrank into herself, ignored him. Of course, he couldn't let her go, she still 'owned' the property even though he managed it. She was on her own. Her mum and dad were gone. It's isolation isn't it, isolation that does so much harm. If you've no-one to turn to, what choice do you have? I think it's better nowadays. There's organisations aren't there? It should help, maybe, but who knows?"

"But do you think your gran knew what he did to your mum?"

"I don't think so. She was such a shadowy figure, it's hard to know for sure. But I've told myself she didn't. I've told myself that, because if she did, well, it makes it even worse."

"How awful it's been for you, Terry."

"I coped. I thought I'd coped well to be honest. Especially since he's been ill. I thought I'd won. I had the run of his property, I had access to a lot of the money. Even though he signs the papers, the flat is decent, better than decent, to be honest. It's one of the ones he owns, but eventually it'll be mine. I thought I was doing okay. Then you came, you came with that bloody piece of paper, and to be honest I saw that it was all built on sand. He was going to get away with unspeakable things, and I hadn't done anything, and once he was dead, that would be the end of it. When you came to me it was like a slap in the face. No, it was much more than that. It made me see that if I let him die…"

He turned now to look at the old man who was shuffling in the chair, trying to turn and see them.

"If I let him die without answering for what he's done, then it would haunt me for the rest of my life. Regret. It would eat away at me. I had someone else to avenge, is that too strong a word, Lily?"

All she could do was to shake her head.

Clive Robertson drew their attention. He wasn't impossible to understand, in fact Lily was surprised how ordinary he sounded. Yes, the words were slurred a little, the delivery was slow, but that was all. "Terry, who's this? Who have you brought?"

Terry looked steadily into Lily's eyes. She could tell that he wasn't about to waste any time, that he was here for one reason and he was getting straight down to business. He pulled an envelope from the pocket of his trousers. He pulled out the two sheets of paper, separated them and unfolded one of them. He walked over to the old man in the chair and held out the DNA report.

Chapter 34

Clive Robertson reached out with a wrinkled, age-spotted hand. "Glasses, glasses!" He nodded and wagged his hand towards a small table positioned beside his chair. Terry leaned forward and picked up the pair of spectacles and handed them over.

The old man turned the paper, examined the back. A frown creased his forehead. "What's this?"

Terry spoke quietly, "Just read it."

"I don't know what it is. Is it from the lawyers?"

"No, just read it."

Clive turned and tipped his chin towards Lily. "Who's this? What the hell is going on today? What are you up to, boy?"

Lily saw Terry clench his hands into tight fists at his sides.

"This is Lily. She's a friend of mine. She came with me today because…"

It seemed to occur to Terry, quite suddenly, that he couldn't really explain why she was there. He glanced at her, frowned, and then stepped nearer to the old man. He took the sheet of paper into his own hand. He leaned down and pointed at the typing.

"This, this is the proof of what you've done. This…"

He jabbed at a point on the page.

"This is your son, and this…"

More jabbing with his finger.

"This proves it beyond any real doubt. This proves that you had a child, a boy. And this…!" Terry's face was reddening now, his voice becoming a little louder, the words clipped and angry. "This is the proof of who was the boy's mother."

He couldn't continue. Lily watched him struggle, there was nothing she could do to help. Silence fell, except for the harsh rattle of Clive Robertson breathing, and the quiet whisper of wind in the trees outside. Rain shushed against the window.

The old man lifted the paper close to his face, he peered at the writing, turned his head, and stared for one long moment at his son. His eyes were empty of the shock and emotion that should have been there. All there was to see was irritation in his small movements. He cast aside the paper and blew out a puff of breath through pursed lips. And in that moment Lily understood. She saw the hardness, the lack of any sort of concern or guilt. She saw what he was and understood that he would have been able to frighten and control a small child, a lonely woman, and a terrified girl.

He reached for the paper where it lay on his lap, ripped it in half, tore it again and again and again, until all that was left were shreds and pieces and he tossed them aside.

"Load of nonsense. Nothing but an inconvenience," he stumbled over the word, tangling it in his damaged mouth. He pressed on, "I dealt with it. If he's turned up now send him on his way. I owe him nothing. I did what was best." He turned with an impatient shrug of his shoulders, stared at the window, watching the drops racing downwards, unmoved, and unafraid.

Terry looked at the pile of paper scraps and then glanced at Lily. There was nothing she could say.

He bent and gathered it all together, grasped hold of the old man's wrist and pushed the debris into his upturned palm.

"No. No, that's not what we're doing. You're not getting away with this anymore." Terry pushed his second piece of paper towards the man's face. "Granddad! Oh no, that's not quite right is it, *Dad*." The final word was loaded with pain. Terry reached and pulled a small footstool towards him. He placed it directly in front of the old man's chair and perched on it. He leaned forward, resting his forearms across his knees and stared directly into the twisted face. "I don't want to discuss this with you, back and forth, debating what is and isn't true. I don't want to hear anything you might have to say about this. I don't even want to be here with you, breathing the same polluted air. What I am going to do…" He stopped.

From where she stood, Lily could see his hands shaking, she could see the gleam of anger in his eyes. She was afraid. Afraid that he wouldn't be able to finish what he needed to say before emotion got the better of him. She wanted to lay a hand on his shoulder, to give him strength, to let him know that he was not alone. But the atmosphere between the two men held her in place, kept her silent.

Clive tipped his head to one side, a small smile twisted the thin, pale lips, his drooping facial muscles contorted. Lily gulped, she had her hands clasped together and felt the nails dig into the soft skin of her palms. She was immobile, didn't want the old man to remember she was there. He was worn down by disease, and reduced by age, but she felt the power emanating from him. The strength of his ego, his confidence. She closed her eyes briefly.

When she opened them, Terry had regained control and was speaking again, quietly, clearly, "Let me tell you what's going to happen now. I'm going to print out more copies of those reports. Both of them." Clive lifted his chin in reaction, Terry nodded before continuing. "Oh come on, even you must know I can make any number of copies. I can print them off over and over and over and you can tear them up as many times as you like, but they'll still be there. Did you really think I would be stupid enough to give you the original? So, I'm taking them to the police. I'm taking them to the papers, I'm probably even going to take them to the bloody Masons, I can send them a copy – should I do that? – should I?"

There was a flicker of something that could have been anxiety, the prospect of shame amongst his peers, the only thing to have evoked anything approaching the reaction Lily had been expecting.

Terry was still speaking, "This is the last time I'm going to come here old man. The next time you see me will probably be in court. And then it will be all out in the open. The disgusting things you did to me, the things you made me do to you. The truth about Mum and the baby that you sold. All of it, and then, you'll pay." He leaned back and prepared to stand.

Clive Robertson coughed, snorted and began to speak. He gripped the chair armrests, his own arms tense and shaking, bony knuckles white under loose, papery skin. "You won't do that. You won't do anything like that. I know you Terrance." It was the first time she had heard his given name and Lily could tell from Terry's reaction that it was a deliberate barb. "I know you. You won't risk your easy life, your car and your flat, and your wages. You do anything with this…" He moved now and threw the shreds of paper back towards Terry. His hand was weak, the result was a flutter of white bits onto the blanket across his knees. It spoilt the effect he had been aiming for, and with a huff of impatience he swept them aside.

"You tell anyone about this garbage and I'll cut you off, without a penny. I'll take back the flat, have you evicted. What are you going to do then – huh? What will you be? You've got no qualifications, no experience, except running around after me. Lap dog, that's what you are, my lap dog. Bought and paid for. And how do you think you'll be treated, eh? How do you think people will look at you? 'Why didn't you say something before now?' That's what they'll say. Taking advantage of a poor sick man who can't stick up for himself. Telling lies to get your hands on the money. Jumping on the bandwagon of all the other cases. Don't be ridiculous. Take this nonsense." He pointed a quaking finger towards the floor. "And take this bloody witness, if that's what she is, and bugger off. Get out, get out, and don't come back until I send for you."

He leaned against the chair back, his physical strength was spent but his eyes were hard, and his mouth twisted into a sneer as he glared at them both.

Terry had taken all he could. He turned to Lily, raised his eyebrows in question, she nodded and then walked before him to the door. She paused, stood for a moment staring forward.

"Are you alright?" He placed his hand on her shoulder.

She nodded, stood for a moment longer before reaching for the door handle, and then they left the room. They stepped back down the great staircase and out into the damp and breezy day.

As they walked to the car, Lily leaned on the arm that Terry had offered. She could feel the thud of blood through her veins, pounding in the back of her head. Once in the car she struggled to control her breathing and rubbed at her chest.

"Are you alright, Lily? I shouldn't have subjected you to that."

"It was my idea. I'm alright. Well, I will be in a minute." She opened her bag and took out one of the pills to calm her down. "Are you alright, Terry? That was awful for you. I don't know what I was expecting, but he is so much worse than I could have imagined."

"Lily, why did you come today? It was so odd, in there I realised that I hadn't really understood. I mean, I just thought it would be good from my point of view to have someone there with me, but why did you agree to come?"

She shook her head and answered him in little more than a whisper, "I think I was looking for Peter. I've always wondered what he would have been like. I just wanted to see him, Peter's father. But apart from that I wanted to be with you. I started this, you were coping and I spoiled that for you. It was too hard for you to do on your own."

That was all she needed to tell him, the rest of it was for her and her alone.

Chapter 35

Terry looked at his watch. "It's nearly two o'clock. We haven't eaten yet. Do you want to go with me and have some lunch?"

Lily nodded. She didn't know when or if she would see him again and under what circumstances. At least this could be a memory, not altogether happy, but with him at least.

He started the car and glanced around before speaking again, "I can't be too long, I have a couple of meetings this afternoon. Just some leases to sign and what have you, but it has to be done."

"So, you're going to keep on working for him?"

They were nearing the end of the drive, he slowed and then stopped between the iron gates.

"I don't have much choice. He's right, I don't have anything else. He had me out of school as soon as he could, and then brought me into working for him."

He paused until he had pulled out onto the narrow road heading back to Bath.

"I didn't mind to be honest. I had trouble dealing with strangers, back then, when I was younger. At least with him I knew what I was getting and he was leaving me alone. You know, all that stuff had stopped. I like the work. It's mainly organising, agents, contractors and what have you. I can do a lot on the phone and, being the owner, you are automatically on top, aren't you? I don't know what I'd do if I didn't do this and I always told myself it would be mine one day. Might not work out quite that way now, but it still has to be kept going. Some things I'd like to do differently. But he won't have any changes, and his solicitor keeps a tight rein on things. Between the two of them they clip my wings a bit."

"When are you going to the police?"

"I'm going to find a solicitor first. Not his, obviously. Not even one from around here, I can't risk that it would be someone he knows. I need to find one with experience of handling this sort of stuff. I think I'm going to have to start with one of those agencies, the helpline things."

"So, you haven't started anything yet?"

He turned quickly and looked at her, gave her a wry grin. "I think I just did, didn't I?"

She nodded and touched his hand briefly. "You were very brave."

"I was very angry. Anyway, it's on the way now. I wanted to do it this way, so there was no chance of bottling it. I've told him, so there's no way back. Now I just have to keep on going. I'll let you know what's happening at every stage. I still wish there was a way to keep your name out of it."

"Don't worry about me, Terry, just do whatever you have to do." As she spoke she felt a quick spark of guilt. It was damped down by the knowledge that she was going to do the right thing, the only thing, that would sort this out once and for all. For all of them.

He nodded. "Right, I know a nice little restaurant, not too far from the station, what time is your train?"

"I bought an open ticket."

"Good. Good, we'll have lunch and then I'll take you into town."

She managed to eat a salad, she had a glass of wine, because he wanted to buy her one, and she felt some of the tension lift.

After the nursing home visit, she was beset with doubts about her ability. Clive Robertson was so much stronger and more able than she had anticipated. She had thought of a weak, partially incapacitated old man and, though he was certainly not fit, neither was she. No matter, she would enjoy this couple of hours and then take things as they came. The decision was made.

She lifted her glass. "Good luck Terry. I know you'll be alright. You will."

He raised his glass in response and nodded. He smiled at her. Even though he was not the Peter of her imagination, she saw now that he was all she would have hoped for, and more besides.

All those years ago, there had been a sacrifice required to save the baby. In the end, they had been found wanting, and their own fear of exposure, and their self-interest had stood in the way of what was right. That wasn't going to happen now. Charlotte Mary would have judged her insane. But then, when it came to it, hadn't she destroyed everything they had by her actions? She was gone, and this was Lily's decision, and it was made.

All too soon the little interlude was over. He glanced at his watch and sighed.

"Are you in a hurry?" She began to gather up her things.

"Well a bit, yes, I have some stuff to do. If you don't mind…"

She tapped him on the arm. "You go, I know you're busy, there's really no need to delay any longer."

"Are you sure?"

"Yes, of course. Off you go. I'll be alright, it's not far from here."

She watched as he drove away. She raised a hand to wave, but he didn't look back and she felt rather foolish standing on the roadside watching his car disappear into the traffic. When she was sure there was no chance of him coming back she turned and walked into town, past the station. It wasn't far to the hotel that she had booked into earlier in the day. She collected her key and went up to her room. She would rest now. There was a kettle and things to make a drink, she had all she needed for the moment.

Chapter 36

Timing was important, vital, so Lily set an alarm. After she woke, she made a drink, took a shower, then dressed in the same clothes as before – they had to recognise her at The Grange.

The hotel reception was empty, so she rang the bell. Almost immediately a young woman appeared behind the counter.

Lily smiled at her. "I wonder," she said, "could you call a taxi for me?"

"Yes, of course, madam. Where are you going?"

"The Grange. It's a nursing home, just outside town. I don't know the area I'm afraid."

"I'm sure the driver will know it. What name is it?"

"Bowers. My name is Lily Bowers."

She moved to a low leather settee in an alcove beside the front door. Her heart was thundering, her throat dry. She began to count slowly backwards from a hundred. She concentrated on the rhythm of the numbers in her mind, struggled to slow her breathing and fought against the claws tightening across her chest.

When the taxi arrived, the driver didn't bother to get out of the car, he blew the horn and turned to her as Lily slid into the back seat. "The Grange is it, love?"

"Yes. Do you know it?"

"I do. Fasten your belt."

As she fumbled with the buckle, he drew away and out into the early evening traffic. Lily leaned her head against the seat back and watched the reflection of the shops and street lamps flashing past in the car windows, projected and slightly distorted on the glass. She was floating, watching herself from above, unreal and unattached. It wasn't unpleasant and she didn't fight against it. It was calming.

She hadn't realised that her eyes had closed and was startled when the driver disturbed her half sleep. He had pulled to the centre of the road and was indicating, ready to turn. She glanced around her.

"Here we are love. Up to the front door, is it? Only, you didn't say. It's not the nurses' lodging you want?"

"No, that's right, the front door. Lovely."

"Will you be wanting a ride back?"

"Oh, I suppose I will, yes." Her mind had not gone further than the task in front of her, but of course there might be an afterwards.

"There's a card on the back ledge, just ring that number. Ask for Mike, that's me. You have to phone and book. Regulations, you know."

"Thank you so much, Mike." She tipped him generously and then, as a final thought, she turned back and leaned towards the taxi. "What time is it please?"

"It's just after six."

That was all that she could do. It ought to be enough, to ensure that she was remembered.

As she pushed open the front door she waved a hand in greeting at the receptionist. "Hello, hello. I'm really sorry. I know it's not visiting time or anything, but I was here earlier with my friend."

"Yes, I remember. Are you feeling better now?"

"I am, thank you. I feel so foolish though. I was so befuddled earlier, and when we left Clive, I forgot my spectacles. We'd been having such a time, looking at some old photographs, and I put them on the table. It wasn't until I needed them later that I realised how careless I'd been."

"Oh, don't worry, I'll just ring for someone."

"No, no, don't do that. I'll just pop up there and collect them." She gave a little laugh. "It'll give me another chance to see him."

"Have you known him for a long time?"

She nodded. "We go back a very long way."

"Well, he will probably be in bed now. He has his dinner in his room."

Lily flapped a hand and chuckled. "Oh, he won't mind. I'm sorry about this. You must be getting ready to go home as well. I don't want to be a bother. Look, let me just pop up there and collect my specs. I'll maybe sit with him a while, if he's not too tired, and then I'll leave him alone." She allowed her face to grow solemn. "I don't know if I'll get another chance to come and see him. I live quite a long way from here and, well as you saw earlier today, I'm not terribly well."

It was enough. The receptionist's natural kindness, combined with her wish to finish her shift tipped the balance. "Alright Mrs erm…"

"Miss, Miss Bowers, Lily."

"The front door will be locked when I leave, so if you just use that side corridor…" She pointed in the direction of a narrow hallway. "The night-time entrance is about halfway along."

"Thank you so much. You are terribly kind. Clive is fortunate to be here while he's not well."

She took her time on the stairs, leaning on the banister and turning to watch as the receptionist locked the front door, and with a final glance towards Lily, left the entrance hall.

The lights had been subdued and the bustle of the day had quieted.

Lily stood for a moment in front of Clive's room. She reached out and pushed the door open just a crack, the way that Terry had done on their visit earlier in the day. Clive was propped in his bed with a mound of pillows around him. He stared forward, and the sound of the television news murmured in the background. A small table on casters had been prepared with cutlery and a drink. The jangle of the meal service drew nearer and Lily glanced around. She must take care now, the last thing she needed was to burst in on another patient.

She pushed at the door of the room next to Clive's, just a crack. A woman sat at a table in the window bay, a shawl around her shoulders, the table in front of her set for dinner. There was only one door on the opposite side of the corridor. She opened it to find linens and cleaning equipment. There were shelves along three sides with a narrow space between. The light switched on automatically. There was a step stool, folded, leaning against the shelving unit. Quietly she opened it out and perched on the narrow top rung. She lowered her head into her hands and let out the breath that she had been holding ever since the first glance into Clive's room. She was beset again by dizziness. This was new, a progression of her symptoms. She must hold herself together for just a little longer. She closed her eyes and listened to the muted sounds out in the hallway.

Now all she could do was wait.

Chapter 37

After a couple of minutes the light went out. Lily imagined that if she moved it would flash back on. It was very tempting. Though the space was small and smelled of fresh laundry and cleaning fluids, it was unnerving to sit in the darkness. But she heard movement outside. Leakage of brightness under the door may give her away. She froze, breathing in small, shallow puffs.

There came the quiet hum of wheels on parquet floor and then a gentle knock. She listened to the exchange of greetings, a clatter of plates and then the same thing repeated a few moments later. It wasn't difficult to imagine the scene and she squeezed her eyes shut and pictured the corridor, the meal service.

Timing, this was all about timing.

In the dark of the linen cupboard she thought of Terry, she thought of Peter, and what could have been, what was lost. She drove back all thought of what she was planning to do. If she allowed her mind to travel that road, the potholes and stumbles would become all too clear, and she could not allow herself to be dissuaded. She was here, the solution to it all was in her hands.

How long? He had to eat the meal. The dining staff would clear it. Would there then be a visit to settle him down? She must allow for that. She remembered the routines in the hospice with Charlotte Mary. This would probably be similar, a little more refined for certain, but the medical requirements of this sort of place must surely be very much the same.

While the corridor was quiet she risked a movement. Just her arm waved in the air, and the light flashed into brightness. Using the shelving for support she lowered herself slowly to the floor. Her back was tight with pain. She pulled a bundle of sheets down beside her, and rested her behind on the welcome softness. Leaning against the wooden frame she was much more comfortable. Again, she waited.

More than an hour passed. She had checked her watch when she shifted her position. After the return of the trolley, the clearing of dishes, she risked the light once more. At last the quiet thud of rubber soles moved along the space outside, the mumble of night-time conversation. She heard again the door, the greeting, and she breathed a small sigh of relief that she had waited, difficult as it had been. She listened for the second door to close and then, the retreating footsteps.

She pushed painfully to her feet. Light flashed bright in the small space and dazzled her. She closed her eyes. The flutter in her chest became a thump and then, as she had known it would, it became a lump of pain. She lowered herself to the top step of the little ladder and rested. She breathed slowly and waited for the tension to ease, the disease to retreat.

How long? He was old, he was sick. Terry had told her that he slept often, they most probably dispensed sleeping pills, so probably not too long. She must act before any night watch made their rounds.

She pushed open the door. The corridor was dimmed and empty. She spun around and checked again. The notice on the back of the door in Clive's room had showed an escape route. She hadn't had a chance to memorise it completely. Terry had fussed and worried when she had stopped. But the red line led to the exit at the end of the corridor and she assumed that there was access to the outside. It was the only thing that made sense. It would be alarmed, she had no doubt, but she would deal with that as it happened. After all, the *afterwards* was only to buy her some time. To win the chance to take care of the other things. If it happened that it went wrong tonight, then half of a success was better than doing nothing and living with yet more regret.

She had so little to lose now and Terry had so much to gain. She would be brave and strong, and take what came. Her bag, slung across her body for safety, held the cache of pills so her escape was assured, either one way or the other. It mattered little which it was to be.

Three steps took her across the corridor. She put the side of her head against the door, listening. The nursing home was still. Not even the distant sound of a television or radio disturbed the quiet. She glanced at her watch. It was after nine. Much later than she had thought.

From inside the room she heard the low rumble of a snore. A smile stretched her mouth. She waited until Clive breathed again, the noise regular and reassuring.

She pushed at the door.

The mound of pillows had been removed and he lay on his side. The covers were pulled close to his face. There was a small night-light plugged into a socket by the wall. The heavy curtains were caught back with a rope tie, but blinds had been lowered part of the way over the windows. It was dim but not too dark.

She moved forward, he didn't stir.

She stopped beside the bed and looked down at him. His face was crushed against the one pillow that had been left under his head. His thin hair was dishevelled and disturbed. A drool of saliva tracked from the sagging lips, across the wrinkled cheeks. The rattle of his snores was loud now that she was so close. She could see nothing of Terry in him, though they had proof that he was imprinted on both of his son's genetic makeup.

Lily bent to the chair drawn up beside the bed, she reached to the small pile of daytime bedding.

It would soon be over. She gasped as her heart jinked and she felt the flutter as it fought to resume a regular rhythm.

She grasped the bulk of the pillow and moved closer. She braced her feet slightly apart on the floor and drew in a deep breath, gathering what strength she had.

Chapter 38

Her instinct was to pounce, to take him by surprise and trust to shock and strength alone. But she had thought long and hard about this. He was drugged, she didn't know how heavily, but his sleep would be deeper than otherwise. Though he was depleted by the effects of the stroke and age, he would still possibly be stronger than she was when he was fighting for his life, struggling for the next breath. Surely, he would call upon every reserve in his body.

Physical activity left her weak and hurting, on top of that was the emotional strain. So, she must be clever.

She swallowed hard. Now was the last moment to pull back. She could call a halt, sneak away into the night, but it was never an option. This was for Terry, and for Peter. Terry had said that shaming his grandfather and exposing his evil would have to be enough, but it wasn't true. He had to pay and there must be no risk to Terry's future, he had earned it and he must have it.

She leaned closer to him, and gently, slowly, lowered the pillow towards his face. It touched his skin and she tensed, waiting for a reaction. There was nothing. She laid it more evenly across his head. He didn't stir. Now, she placed her hands flat on the edges, she bent towards him.

She applied more pressure. She didn't know what to expect, but there must be something, surely.

His legs moved under the covers, she felt him tense, felt the push of his shoulders and head upwards, against the pillow. She leaned yet more heavily. His feet moved now, back and forth. His arms tensed and strained under the bedclothes. She lifted herself on her toes, lay across the bed, trapped his upper body under the covers. His legs kicked out, his head shifted under the weight of down and feather, she slid fully onto the bed, completely stretched across him, pinning his head and shoulders with her own body. She reached to the other side of the bed, grasped at the edge of the mattress, locking herself across him with the weight of her legs on one side and the clutch of her hands on the other. He bucked against her a couple of times.

She squeezed her eyes tightly shut, held her breath and willed her weight to hold him, pressing into the mattress, closing off any chance of the pillow sliding.

She felt his head move again, and again and she heard him. It wasn't a groan, just a small sound, an expiration of air, and then he stilled. She lay across him, waiting.

How long? If it was too soon he would wake and cry out, and she would have failed. How would she tell if it was done? She waited, began to breathe, began to cry. Still she waited.

Time was endless and immeasurable, she thought he breathed, then knew that he had not.

She uncurled her hands from the edge of the mattress, began to slide back across the bed, her feet reaching for the floor. She stood, bent at the waist, constantly pressing down, still alert to any movement. There was none. She rested her feet flat on the floor, leaning heavily with her arms and then, slowly, she began to straighten. He was still.

She took in a great gulp of air. Released the pressure. Waited. He was still.

His hand was visible under the disturbed bedding. She touched it. Nothing. She pulled at his fingers and felt no reaction. Garnering all her will power she lifted up the pillow.

His eyes were closed. His mouth gaped open, as if it were still possible to draw in air but his lips were blued. She poked at his face.

It was done, she knew it was over. Lily replaced the pillow on top of the others. She lowered her head to his face, her ear to his mouth. She waited for a whisper of breath that didn't come. She reached with her fingers and felt at his neck, as she remembered the nurses doing when Charlotte Mary had finally gasped her last. She could feel no flutter of life. She picked up his hand and let it drop. It fell lifeless and heavy onto the bed.

She had killed.

She was a murderer.

But it had been so calm compared to the poor baby, the desperate attempts to drip fluid into his tiny mouth. The awful last moments when they had watched the rapid flutter of his chest as it rose and fell, rose, and fell and didn't rise again. This was too easy. She didn't believe he had even been aware of his body's reaction, the kicking of his legs, the straining for breath had been nothing more than instinct. It wasn't enough, he hadn't been afraid, he had simply slept through a dream and not emerged into the morning.

She pushed him, shook his shoulders, lifted his lifeless hand again and let it drop.

Her hands covered her mouth as she backed away from the bed. Staring at his dead face, at the disturbed covers, her eyes grew round with horror and fear.

A sound in the night brought her back to herself. It was an owl in the garden, or the woods beyond the wall. Time reset itself and she stepped back to the bed. Thoughts tumbled and rolled, there were things she must do. She glanced around the room. All was as it had been when she entered, a lifetime ago. She pulled back the covers and with a heave she rolled him over, he should face away from the door so that anyone looking in would see only the back of his head. She straightened the lie of his limbs and dragged the bedclothes over him, up to his neck.

She listened, the night was quiet, the nursing home still.

She had done it.

Chapter 39

Lily took one last look at the bed, and the body. Backing away from the awful scene, she glanced around the dim room and came to a halt in front of the notice about fire exits. She used the glare of white light on her phone to examine the plan.

She pulled the door open a little and listened to the silence. Once she was as sure as she could be that the corridor was empty, she left without a final glance behind.

It was a couple of dozen steps and quickly achieved. The door was heavy wood with wired glass in a small pane at head height. Probably just opening it would cause a bell or a siren to sound and mayhem would ensue. She could find no notice or warning. She turned her head and peered back down the corridor.

She considered hiding somewhere for the rest of the night but no, she would flee. She didn't truly expect to avoid detection, she had taken many steps to ensure that she had been noted. But that was so there would be no chance of suspicion falling on Terry. When they searched for the guilty party she had to be the obvious and only possibility. Nevertheless, now it came to it, she was driven to get away, to go home, even though it may very well be for one last time. She reached for the metal bar and pushed open the door.

There was no scream of sound, no cacophony of bell and siren. She stepped through and onto a wide top step. The stairs were concrete and the walls decorated with cream paint. The door swung closed behind her with a quiet thud. She turned through ninety degrees and then clung to the metal banister. She descended the staircase, her ears straining, waiting for the cry behind her. Of course, the alarm may have been silent, a flashing light in some small office, manned by uniformed security men. Nothing happened and she pressed on.

At the bottom of the narrow flight there was another door, and on this one was the notice she had been expecting. Above the grab bar, the stark warning that 'This Door Is Alarmed.'

She stretched a hand out and then paused. She wasn't clear whereabouts this door was in relation to the main drive and the grand front entrance. It would be tucked around the side, but it could open into a yard with fences and gates, a slope that would take her falling and rolling into a heap. But, no, it was a fire escape so surely there would be safety beyond it. She wouldn't be able to run, it had been a long time since she could do much more than stroll, but it could be possible to hide. She glanced back into the gloom, there was no help up there.

Where she stood was a tiny hallway with a flagged floor. She shone the phone light around. In the corner was a small pile of cigarette ends. They told their own tale. A place to be away from the ubiquitous smoke alarms. A place for staff to hide out of the weather and feed their addiction.

She thrust a hand into her bag. In the very bottom, she felt the smooth hardness. Back in the day they had both smoked, cigarettes and roll ups with marijuana threaded through the tobacco. Charlotte Mary had bought those gold lighters and fancy, jewelled cases. She had this for no other reason than habit. Though it was years since she had used it for the original purpose, it had been something she transferred from bag to bag, like her wallet and her keys.

She bent and picked up one of the bigger pieces of discarded cigarette, and cleared the bits of dust away with her thumb. She pushed the squashed end back into shape and put the filter tip between her lips. She flicked the lighter; at first it refused to ignite. She held it up to her ears and shook it. She felt, rather than heard, the swill of fuel inside it. She flicked it again. There was a small spark. She held it between her hands, warming it. She flicked it again, and a tiny flame quivered in the draught. She lit the cigarette and inhaled the scented smoke. It was horrible. Had they really believed this was pleasant? She felt a cough begin to tickle, and took the thing out of her mouth.

She cleared her throat, then leaned and thumped upwards on the metal bar. As the door swung open a flashing red light lit the hallway. Lily stepped out onto a path. There was no clatter of a bell, not yet. So, a silent alarm was illuminated somewhere. No need to upset and frighten sick people, not until the threat was assessed.

She threw the glowing cigarette end onto the step, dragged the door closed and then scuttled along the narrow path in the direction of the lights along the drive.

She heard the thud of running feet, didn't dare to look back. There was a bin store here, it was locked. But at the side furthest from the building was a place to crouch in the dark. Her heart was pounding painfully and sweat popped out onto her forehead, cooling quickly in the night air. She shivered and dropped to her knees, supporting herself with two hands against the wooden sides of the storage space.

The guard appeared, his torch lighting the narrow path, his feet thundering towards her, past her. He skidded to a halt by the fire door and shone the beam of a huge flashlight back and forth across the expanse of grass, along the length of the walls. He touched the glowing cigarette with the toe of his boot. He took out his radio. "Jack?"

She heard the crackle of a response.

"I'm at the eastern fire door. Door's closed now. You check the interior. But there's a bloody fag end here. This is the third time this month. I'm writing it up this time. Bloody hell, they've got their soddin' smokers' shelter, but do they use it? Do they buggery."

Another hiss of a reply.

"Okay, I'll meet you in the stairwell but I don't think we have a problem here. I'll tell you what though if I find who this is, bloody heads are going to roll."

He pushed again at the fire door and then turned and retraced his steps along the path and vanished around the corner.

Lily dug into her bag to find the medicine spray and then flopped onto her bottom on the damp grass as she waited for her body to calm.

Chapter 40

Lily kept to the grass and shadows along the edge of the drive – in and out between shrubs and trees. She stopped twice, leaning against the rough bark, and gasping for air. The great iron gates were closed, but not locked. There were houses in the distance, but it was too far for her to walk. Already her limbs were heavy and she was weighed down with exhaustion. She would call the taxi. Her phone was in the bottom of her bag and as she pushed her hand inside, she glanced back towards the nursing home.

There were lights approaching in the distance, a familiar shape, and she remembered the bus stop outside the gates of the home. She walked as quickly as she was able, back the few hundred yards. She couldn't yet see the destination board. But it would take her away, and it didn't really matter to where.

The driver barely glanced at her as she clambered aboard. "Town centre please?"

He nodded. "One pound fifty." He gave a puff of impatience as she rooted for her purse, but she found change.

Lily's mind was reeling. When thoughts of the last hour tried to push forward she thrust them away. First of all, she must just breathe. She couldn't think about it. Not yet, not until she was somewhere safe, and alone. She must breathe and fill her mind with stuff, with anything. She lowered her head, opened her bag again, fiddled with the things inside with trembling, dirty fingers. She noticed that her nail beds were tinged with blue. She was not well at all. She looked at her trousers, the knees were wet and muddy. She brushed at them, but the action simply spread the damp dirtiness. She laid the bag across them, but there was no need, there was no-one to hide them from.

She had to occupy her thoughts, mustn't allow the panic in. She took out her tiny diary and flipped through the empty pages, reading notes about holidays and Holy days, concentrating on the print and the colours. She noted the appointment with her doctor, pulled the little pencil from its storage pouch and crossed it out. Red letters, Christmas, the future. She thrust it back into her bag. Thoughts of the future had caused her stomach to flip. She had no future. She had now, and the next few minutes, and maybe the hour after that. Her breathing quickened, she battled against the nerves. She mustn't lose her head now, mustn't let go, not yet.

She thought of Terry, the lunch they had shared. Was it really today? Only hours ago, it didn't seem possible. She thought of his kindness, his pale eyes that held a secret only she was a party to. She and Clive. And now Clive was gone.

With that thought came doubts. Had he truly been dead? How sure could she be? He hadn't moved, she hadn't detected any breathing. But what about after she left, what if the life force hadn't been fully extinguished? Perhaps, even as she had been in the narrow staircase, his heart had convulsed, his lungs expanded and cleared. Could she be sure that there had been no pulse? Had she waited long enough? And if he had stirred, if his body had refused to give up the fight, would he know what had happened? Would he remember through the mists of drugged sleep, the weight of her body, the pillow?

With the thought that maybe he wasn't dead came a jumble of emotions. Relief. Yes, she was not a murderer, she had not taken a life. She was wicked, but she would not have the most dreadful of stains on her soul. But what if he remembered? What if he had been more aware than he had seemed? Well, no matter, she was prepared to be accused, to make the sacrifice so Terry wouldn't lose everything. That had been the reason for it all. If the finger of accusation pointed at her, it would be good. She would have her day in court. She would expose everything, the incest, the evil. She would tell them about Peter, it would be cleansing. Yes, that would be a good thing.

But, surely, he was dead. She had listened close to his face, there had been no breathing. No, no, he was dead.

She felt panic rising up from her stomach, bitter acid, and gulped it down. She turned to the window and concentrated on the flash of lights in the darkness outside as they neared the city. She must hold her nerve. Not much longer.

As the bus pulled into the brightness of the bus station, she gripped the back of the seat, and tried to stand. Her knees were water, her legs shook and her arms began to tremble. She breathed deeply, took a moment to gather her strength and then, using the back of the seats on either side of the aisle, she propelled herself forward. Lily stepped down to the pavement and turned towards the hotel just a short walk away.

The receptionist glanced up and smiled. In the lift, leaning against the mirrored walls the shivering began, and by the time she slipped the key card in and out of the lock, her body was riven with rigors. Tears flooded from her eyes and whimpering sobs escaped her lips.

She fell into the room, pushed the door closed behind her and sank to the floor where she lost herself at last, in horror and fear and shock.

Chapter 41

When she came back to her senses, still on the carpet, just inside the room door, Lily's back and shoulders were stiff and sore. It was cold, and though no longer suffering spasms of shivering, she felt battered and exhausted. She rolled onto all fours, then, gripping at the shelves of the clothes-hanging alcove, pushed as near to upright as her complaining body would allow. She staggered to the bed, kicked off the wet, muddy shoes, and dragged off her filthy trousers.

She swivelled around, lifted her legs to the mattress, and dragged the covers up to her chin. She curled on her side and closed her eyes.

Sleep would not come. Over and over the events rolled through her memory. She tried to focus on the lunch with Terry, but those images would not form. Any feelings of pleasure were obliterated by other emotions: the fear, the horror, and the disgust at what she had done. It occurred to her that, no matter what else happened in the days before she died, she would carry these thoughts with her.

These memories were a part of her being. They were as real as the birthmark on her arm, the wild curls of hair which would have their way in the damp, and the constant sadness at all the precious things that had slipped through her fingers.

She had always thought that the experience with poor, dead Peter would be the worst thing that could ever happen. When Charlotte Mary had died, there had been sorrow, but nothing compared to the emotions experienced at the loss of the baby. Now, these current sensations overwhelmed even that old, never-forgotten pain.

In the still of the dark room it seemed she could hear Clive's final gasping wheeze. She could smell the old man, the stink of his hair, the hospital scent of his bedding. She felt him near her, the thrust of his head against her chest through the pillow. The ghost of his body tensing and bucking against hers.

She cried out, sat up. She heard a siren in the distance, coming nearer. Someone else in trouble, but there could be no greater trouble, surely, than what she had brought upon herself.

She leaned forward, bent her knees, and wrapped her arms awkwardly around them. She swayed back and forth in the bed, whimpering quietly. And then, she thought of Terry, of Peter, of Carol Robertson, and the panic subsided a little. She remembered the restaurant, his kindness and consideration, and reminded herself why she had done it.

For Terry, to protect him from himself. It wasn't right that he should risk losing everything to that evil old man. For them all, so that he wouldn't have any chance of being pardoned for the unforgivable. He was old, the wheels of justice could likely roll so slowly that his life would have come to a peaceful and natural end, before there was any sort of reckoning. Or if he lived and stood trial, what would they do? The old judges, the clever lawyers. Maybe they would incarcerate him in a low security place and, for him, already confined by his failing body, it would have been no punishment.

She had done it for Peter, conceived in brutal misery, sold as an inconvenience, and condemned to a life so short that he never even learned to smile.

And her, how much of the sadness in her own life could be laid at the door of Clive Robertson. If he had never touched them, if Charlotte Mary had never brought home Carol's innocent child, then surely their own lives would not have been ruined the way they had been. So much of it could be traced back to what had happened in that broken family. Charlotte Mary carried some of the guilt, of course she did, but if the child hadn't been available, then the story would have had no beginning.

She was calmer now. It had begun to make sense to her, the way it had when she had planned it. She had committed a great sin, but she must own it now and acknowledge the truth. Clive Robertson had not deserved to live, and she had rid the world of his malign influence.

She threw back the covers and walked across the room to the little dresser. She began to make a cup of tea and, while she waited for the kettle to boil, she stripped off the rest of her stained clothes and wrapped herself in the dressing gown she had brought with her. It smelled of home and comforted her with the familiar.

After the drink was finished she didn't lie down but sat, quietly, propped against the pillows. When she closed her eyes, the images were kinder. Her mother and father, school concerts and the early days with Charlotte Mary, the loving and the laughter and of course she thought of Terry. She dozed and relaxed and allowed herself to let go of the anguish.

* * *

The thump of feet along the corridor outside her door woke her. At first, she was disoriented, she didn't remember falling asleep. Then the events of the previous day flooded her mind. She regarded them calmly.

She would do her best not to spend her final days tormented with guilt because of a wicked, twisted man. He had already stolen too much from her and the other people he touched. She would do as much as she could to live in the moment and if, when she died, there was any sort of reckoning, she would accept it, because she had done what she did for reasons that made sense, that were just, and necessary.

She wished that she could see Terry, but it probably wasn't possible. Not today. His day was to be unlike any other and there wouldn't be space in it for her.

She heard another siren, it slowed at the junction near the hotel, and for a moment she was startled. Of course, she may not have the chance to get back to Southsea. If they found her before then, she would never see her home again. It made her sad, but the new-found calmness prevailed. If that was to be the way of it, well, it didn't matter so much – although it would be nice to sit with Peter one last time and tell him that soon his brother would come for him. She thought of the letter waiting for Terry, and the things that would happen once she was gone. She hoped that he would understand and that, understanding, he would carry out her wishes. But there was a limit to the little power she had, and his actions in the future were beyond her control.

She packed her few things together and went down to the dining room. Two big cups of coffee and a plate of eggs and toast were only slightly spoiled by the need to constantly glance at the reception area, waiting for the police. But nobody came, no uniforms appeared and it seemed that she would get home after all.

* * *

In the two hours it took for the journey, Lily found herself plunging back into fear and despair. She had accomplished the thing that she had set out to do, and what a dreadful thing it was. From this distance of time and space it was unreal, and yet, she knew she had killed.

She knew what must be next. They would come soon and before then she must make sure that everything was in order. Perhaps she had one more day, and maybe one more after that. If it took them a while to find her, then she must put the reprieve to good use. Undoubtedly, things would take their course, a post-mortem, and then investigation. It wouldn't be instant. Impossible to know how long. There were things still in her house needing to be organised, to make life easy for whoever took care of all that.

Of course, when they arrested her, they would search her things. If they searched the cellar they would find evidence of the past weeks, spilled candle wax, scraps of flower petals. What would they think? Anyway, they would see the recent disturbance, from when she had collected the hair. They would dig up the grave and then…

The panic began to build again. Would they take out the tiny body? What would they assume? Some sort of black magic, child abuse, trafficking? Terry would very possibly work out the truth even if he hadn't yet read her letter, but it mustn't fall to him to implicate himself in any way. She must act. Before they came and began any searches she must take care of Peter, make him safe. They mustn't take him away and lay his bones on a table, she had seen it, on the television. They would poke at him with instruments, remove samples, he would become a thing, a laboratory experiment. No, that couldn't be.

Again, she was befuddled by the way that one event led to another urgent task, and another. But then, this was where it had all begun. With Peter and his safety, with his peace.

She turned into her driveway. Sandra's door opened. Had she been lying in wait? Watching from behind the net curtains? "Lily. Have you had a nice break? We noticed you were away. Good idea, the best thing."

Lily painted on a smile, managed a nod. "It was very nice, thank you."

"Well I hope it's done you good. You just have to keep on, don't you? You'll get there."

Lily bit back the obvious question about her supposed destination, pulled her key from the pocket on the front of her bag.

Sandra had come nearer to the hedge, she was speaking again, "Anyway, I won't keep you. I just thought you should know, you've had visitors, while you were away. This morning."

So, they had found her already. Her heart trembled. Had they asked Terry? They must have done, how else could they have detected who she was? And so, she supposed, he was lost to her now. He would draw away. The chance to take care of Peter may be gone. However, she had succeeded in her intention of ensuring there was no suspicion falling on anyone other than herself. She had protected him at least. Sandra was still watching, still smiling.

Lily knew she must speak, "Oh right, thank you, Sandra. I suppose they'll come back if it was important."

"He seemed surprised that you weren't here."

"Did he? Oh well. I'm here now."

"He's very nice, polite. Is he from around here?"

This didn't make sense, the conversation was fractured. "Do you know who it was then, Sandra?"

"Yes, sorry. Oh honestly, I should have said. It was that young man, the one who came the other day. The one I thought was Charlotte's nephew. Do you remember?"

"Ah, oh right, I thought you meant it was…" She stopped. "Terry. You mean Terry."

"Right, well you didn't tell me his name I don't think. Anyway, it was him and he knocked on our door, asked us if we'd seen you. I've been watching for you to be honest. He seemed a bit upset."

Lily took her mobile from her pocket, she glanced at the screen, punched the button on the side and then held it up to show it to Sandra. "Flat, my battery is flat. Oh dear, I expect he's been trying to ring me. Thank you so much, Sandra. I should get inside, plug this in." She waved the phone in the air. "I'll give him a call."

"Right, yes. Well, pop round some time. We'll have a cup of tea. A chat."

"I will, thank you. Yes, I will."

She dropped her bags beside the front door and rushed to the kitchen where the phone charger lay on the worktop. There were three text messages. All this morning. All from Terry:

I need to speak to you. It's urgent. I have tried your phone but it goes to voicemail. And then just a few minutes later: *I am coming to Southsea. If you get this will you call me?*

And the final one, just over an hour ago:

I have been to your house. I spoke to the neighbours. She said you were away. I'll stay around for an hour or so but then I must get back. Please, please call me if you get this message.

Chapter 42

Had she missed him? She snatched up the phone and dialled. "Terry, is that you?" But it wasn't, it was his voicemail. She gabbled her message, "I've only just come in. My phone battery was flat. I'm so sorry. Can you call me when you have a chance? I'm here now."

She paced back and forth in the hallway. The phone was on the small table, charging. She picked it up whenever she was within reach, even though it hadn't chimed, the screen hadn't lit. She was afraid to leave it, couldn't take it with her because the charge was still so low. All her attention was focused on the tiny screen. When it rang, she started with shock, though it was just what she had been waiting for. His name was on the display.

"Terry?"

"Yes. Lily, are you at home now? I need to talk to you and I don't want to do it on the phone. I was on my way back to Bath when I got your call. Look, I'll turn round. I haven't got a lot of time, but I would like to see you. I want to talk to you."

"Yes. I'm in the house now. I'll stay here and wait for you." She knew she should leave it at that, but she couldn't. "What's wrong, Terry? Is there something wrong?"

"Yes, there is. But look, I don't want to talk about it now. I'll be with you in about half an hour."

She replaced the phone and flopped onto the chair. Her eyes fell on the bags, still on the mat near the door. She carted them to the bedroom. She opened the wardrobe to hang up her dressing gown. The dirty trousers and top from yesterday must be thrown away, they went into a refuse bag. Not because she thought of them as evidence, just because she couldn't ever imagine wearing them again.

She looked down at her shoes, they were still muddy. There was dirt on the carpet. She pulled off the offending footwear and carried it downstairs along with the bulging black plastic sack. The clothes went into the bin outside the back door; she placed her shoes on a sheet of newspaper in the kitchen porch, for cleaning later.

She stowed the pills back in the bathroom cabinet, she hadn't needed them after all. It was impossible to imagine that scenario now. Everything had been different from the way she had thought it might be. She had visualised some sort of confrontation with the police. A police cell, a toilet where she would gulp them down. She had imagined it to be like something on the television, but all that had happened was that she had caught a bus, and then this morning enjoyed her breakfast. She laughed, not sure what was amusing her, she giggled again. She tried to stop, to be quiet, but still the laughter bubbled in her stomach. Her throat was tight with tears. She recognised this as the beginnings of hysteria and knew she must stop it. She must not let go. She went into the bathroom and ran cold water over her hands, splashed at her face.

He must be nearly here. She knew of course what he wanted to tell her. It was obvious. How much did he already know? What had they told him, the authorities, whoever he had spoken to? What were they thinking? She would assume that, for the moment at least, he didn't know her part in Clive's death. Surely, if he had, it would be police calling at the door and not him. Or was he coming to warn her?

As if in answer to her thoughts she saw movement beyond the translucent glass in the door, someone walking along the path. She ran to the window and leaned close to the thin blind. The scene outside was vague and smeary. She lifted the corner of the blind and peered out. She was too late, whoever it was had moved beyond her field of vision and under the porch. She wrapped her arms around herself and waited for the bell to ring.

Chapter 43

"Terry. Come in, why are you here? In Southsea, I mean?" She didn't want to lie, but he must be kept at arm's length from the crime. Having no knowledge or suspicion was the only thing that would keep him safe. She was entering yet another world of subterfuge and she hated this one even more than the others. Clive had been evil, Terry was courageous and didn't deserve dishonesty, but it was for his own good.

"I came to see you. I can't stay long but I thought I'd better come in person and let you know."

"I got the impression it was something urgent. Sandra next door told me you'd called earlier."

"I think you should sit down, Lily."

She allowed herself to be ushered through to the living room.

"Right, well." His face was set, there was barely controlled emotion, tension, and excitement in every part of his body. His voice shook, "He's dead."

"What? Who?" More pretence, more lying.

"Clive is dead. They rang me early this morning from the home."

"Well, that was sudden, wasn't it?"

"Yes, I guess so. You were there with me, you heard them, didn't you? They said he was improving. He certainly didn't seem any worse when we were with him. But the thing is…"

She gave him time.

He spoke, quietly, "Well, I have to go and see them later of course, but they said that it was most likely a second stroke. Lily…?"

Still she waited. The less she said the less chance there was that her tongue would trip her.

"Do you think that what we did, what I did, caused him to have another stroke? Do you think it was my fault?"

Her instinct was to offer reassurance, something to help, to still his nerves. She drew her brows together, answered him with a frown of puzzlement painted on her face, "He didn't seem that upset though. He was angry, but I rather got the impression that he was often angry."

"Well, there's no denying that. You're right, that's the way he was, always. When I did things that he didn't agree with, 'stepped out of line' and 'got above myself'." He laughed. "That was one of his favourites! But yes, he didn't seem any worse than normal. Do you think that, maybe afterwards, when we'd gone, maybe he got wound up?"

Lily tried again to calm him, "But if so, wouldn't they know? They must have checked him, surely? You know, taken his blood pressure and what have you? And then if they were concerned they would give him treatment."

She was caught between a chance of self-preservation and concern for Terry's feelings of guilt. She must ease his conscience but then if they thought Clive had a stroke, did that mean there would be no questions? It seemed too good to be true. She had to speak now, find something non-committal.

"I think sometimes these things just happen. When it's time for the end. Will there be a post-mortem?" She had to ask.

"Don't know. They didn't say anything about that. Oh, I don't know what to think just now. I'm all over the place with how I feel. Don't get me wrong, I'm not going to pretend I'm sorry, never that. But it's sudden, a shock. I wasn't ready for this. My mind was on all the other stuff. Anyway, I have to go back now and see them. I must go and see the solicitor. He phoned me as well, they'd rung him to tell him. He and Clive were always close and he visited The Grange a lot. I just wanted to tell you. I don't know what difference it makes to you really, knowing he's gone. Does it help? Does it make you feel any better?"

"Oh, I don't know, Terry. I haven't had time to take it in."

"No, of course you haven't." As he spoke he leaned and squeezed her hand. "Anyway, I just wanted to let you know. I thought it was only right that I come and tell you personally. After all, we do have a sort of connection, don't we? It's an odd, sad connection but – well it makes me think that we have a sort of shared past."

"That's a lovely thing to say, Terry, and I know what you mean, I do. I have wondered many, many times over the years, what Peter would have been like. Well, you already know that. I've come to see, over the last few weeks, that, if he had been like you, his brother, I would have been very proud."

Terry smiled at her, she thought he seemed a little abashed. He was sweet, not at all the person she had originally thought.

"I have to get back. I haven't had time to process much of this yet. It's going to make a difference to a lot of things. One of them is Peter's ashes. How would you feel now about us taking them and putting them with Mum? You know it's an end in a way, so we could do that soon. I could even take them now if you like. It would save me a trip. I'd take you of course, afterwards. When things have calmed down a bit."

Her mind spun. Again, she had been shown a glimpse of something wonderful only to have it snatched away instantly. Once he believed that they had laid his brother to rest, it would be over – she didn't want it to be over, not yet. Apart from the fact that the ashes weren't Peter's, there was of course the other thing, the truth. If she told him about the grave, so near to where they sat, how would he feel about her then?

She wanted to talk to him for longer, to keep him there with her. She asked him the obvious question, "Terry, what about all of that other business, what about Peter? You and Clive? Him and your mum? The things he did. What are you going to do about that now?"

He looked down at his feet and shook his head. "I don't know. Again, I haven't had time yet. I said before that I didn't want him to die before I had the chance to have my revenge, but now, well there's not much I can do about the way it's turned out. I just don't know. I'll have to think about it once I get things sorted out a bit."

Lily answered him quietly, "If there is anything I can do, let me know. Keep in touch won't you, Terry? Let me know what's going on?"

"Of course, I will." He glanced at his watch. His phone rang, he wagged it in the air, mouthed an apology. She nodded and walked from the room to give him space. She stood in the hall, just beyond the door. It was the solicitor, they discussed times.

Terry raised his voice, snapping at whoever was at the other end of the call, "I'll get there as soon as I can, Andrew. I'm sure you realise there are things I've had to do. Yes, yes, I know you're busy. I'm pretty bloody busy myself today. I'll be a couple of hours."

She heard him curse under his breath as he came to find her. "Look, I'll have to go. I'll ring you later if I get the chance."

She stood in the doorway, waved to him as he strode away along the street.

She thought of her stash of pills. Not yet, he still needed her, she couldn't do it yet. She would know when it was time. For now, all she could do was continue with her preparations. First, though, she would go into the basement and tell Peter what had happened.

Chapter 44

The offices in the heart of Bath weren't particularly imposing, but Terry had always felt intimidated when visiting Clive Robertson's solicitors.

When he was very young, confused and frightened by the things that were happening in his life, they made him sit on a hard chair in the corner, his feet swinging between the chair legs. He was bored and constantly afraid that Clive would suddenly whip around and fire a question at him that he would be unable to answer, and they would roar laughing at him. They drank whisky, they told jokes which he didn't understand and afterwards, back in the bustle of the town centre, his grandfather red-faced and a little unsteady, he would breathe a sigh of relief.

Now that he was older, more confident, he could hold his own with the old man, the senior partner, but he would never be totally at ease. The spectre of the small boy watched always from the corner of the room.

Despite the earlier phone call urging him to hurry, he was kept waiting for fifteen minutes in the reception area. When he was eventually ushered into Andrew Stoner's office though, the old wooden desk was bare of paperwork, and Andrew stood before the tall windows which looked out onto a secluded patch of garden.

Terry waited near the door. Neither of them spoke. When he eventually turned, the solicitor simply nodded and pointed to one of the two visitors' chairs that were placed in front of the desk.

Terry knew that to speak first would put him at a disadvantage. He pulled his phone from his trouser pocket and made a display of turning it off. He placed it on the wooden arm of the chair and clenched his hands together on his lap. The silence between them grew.

Terry glanced at his watch, turned to look out of the window, and chalked up a minor victory when Stoner cleared his throat and murmured, "Right, well," and slid open one of the desk drawers.

He spoke again. Though his voice had roughened with age, it still held a shadow of the past and Terry felt his insides lurch. "So, this is a bad day."

Terry didn't respond.

The solicitor opened a file and laid it flat on the desk. "It was very sudden. I was shocked when they called from The Grange."

Terry inclined his head.

"We were friends for a long time. I am saddened by this."

Again, Terry simply nodded. When it became obvious that there was going to be minimal feedback, the solicitor shrugged his shoulders and visibly attempted to settle himself.

"Right, well. I think that over the next few weeks and months, we are going to have a fair amount of work to do. For the moment though there are just the immediate arrangements, I have instructions here about the funeral and burial."

"I'm surprised he's done that," Terry said quietly, keeping his voice steady, "when he began to recover from the first stroke, I tried to talk to him about signing some things over, making sensible arrangements. Letting me take more of the burden. But he just wouldn't hear of it. He said he wasn't about to die yet. Yes, I'm surprised, but I suppose it'll make things simpler."

"He was more comfortable being in charge. It was his way, always."

"Oh yes, I'm aware of that." Terry recognised the barbed comment but was determined not to let it annoy him. He gave a short laugh and was rewarded with a glare from the solicitor.

"I repeat, I've known him a long time. We were friends. We have a long history, since before you were born. I am grieving for my friend today, Terrance, and I'd thank you to remember that. I spoke to him only yesterday. I wish I had known it would be the last time…" He shook his head, took out a large handkerchief and blew his nose.

Terry's mind was racing. This place, this man, were so very much a part of the pain of his childhood that he had kept his contact to a minimum. He'd done as much as he could by telephone or short, fleeting appointments, dealing with a junior partner whenever that was possible, or an assistant. He hadn't given too much thought lately to the bond between Clive and this old man. He realised that they were probably close confidants.

Sitting in the old-fashioned offices, he was only vaguely aware of the wrinkled face in front of him and the drone of Andrew's words as he read out details of funeral directors to be used, the family grave, the one where his gran and mother were. It was garbled and indistinct as his attention focused on the implications of what he had just been told. Words spoken in a moment of passion and without consideration.

He held up a hand. Andrew Stoner stopped mid-sentence, his face puzzled, his mouth a tight line. There was anger, held in check by professionalism, but there was surprise also.

"What?" Stoner snapped out the one word as he let the paper he was holding drop to the desk, and laid his hand on top of it.

"You spoke to him yesterday?" Terry asked.

He huffed now with impatience and shook his head. "Look, I haven't a lot of time, let's just get through this. Terrance, we might as well have our cards on the table, I am well aware that you don't like me. I know how much you resented that your grandfather placed such a great deal of trust in my opinion. I know you feel I had too much influence on his business affairs but, for now, let's just deal with the matters at hand. There will be much to discuss in the coming weeks, but today is not the time for that."

Terry dismissed the rant, the words barely registered. "Why did he call you yesterday?"

A cloud passed through the solicitor's eyes. He tried to take back control. "That is confidential, he was my client. He was my friend."

"No."

"I beg your pardon?" Stoner half rose, braced his hands on the desk and then remembered himself and lowered back to the seat. "Look, we are both a little overwrought. I know your relationship with Clive was difficult at times, but today you must be in shock. You're emotional. Why don't we make another appointment, tomorrow or the day after? I'll have my assistant call you."

"Mr Stoner, why did he call you? What time?"

The old man made a show of glancing at his pocket watch. He tutted. "He called on a private matter."

"You've known him a long time, haven't you? You've known him since before I was born?" Terry asked.

"I worked for him since the year your mother was born. Even before that we were friends." Andrew Stoner's face had reddened, there was a quiver now in the knuckly fingers.

Terry leaned forward towards the desk. "What did he tell you yesterday?"

The office filled with silence.

Chapter 45

Lily snatched up the phone when Terry's number showed on the screen. She listened to his report of the meeting with barely a comment. Only when he fell silent did she speak, "So, he just told you to leave?"

"Yes. After I asked him what Clive had spoken to him about, he said that he didn't have time and he had another appointment. Well, there was nothing much I could do short of making a scene. So, I had to leave."

"Where are you now?"

"I'm at home. I need to go to The Grange in a little while, but I needed to come home first. I needed to calm down. You do see what this means don't you, Lily?"

"I think so."

"Well, to put it bluntly, I reckon he could have been mixed up in a lot of this. I think Clive rang him to warn him. I don't know if he knew about me, I'm trying not to think about it too deeply because he almost certainly does now, and I've got to try and work with him. Oh God, I'll never be able to look him in the eye again."

"Terry, you haven't done anything wrong. You have nothing to be ashamed of."

"Huh, that's easy for you to say, Lily. It's not what it feels like from here. They were so close, he must have known about Peter. He must have known Mum was pregnant, I see now that he must have known why there was no baby afterwards. I bet he knew all of it. Everything. But more importantly, since yesterday, since Clive called him, he must know that I know."

She answered him thoughtfully, "I suppose a lot of it depends on how close they were. I can't believe Clive would tell him about being Peter's father. If he did, this solicitor would have to report it to the authorities, he'd have to. In his position, surely, he'd have to? I expect there was some sort of story, something about an affair, a boyfriend."

"I don't know, I'm not convinced of that. They were close friends all the time I was growing up. Clive used to make me go with him to the office, I hated it. It frightened me, watching them together, being the butt of their jokes."

He paused for a moment. "Something odd though, now I think about it. Andrew never visited, he never came to the house. We didn't see many people it must be said, but you would have thought, wouldn't you, that a close friend like that, he'd have come to see us sometimes? I wonder how much yesterday was a revelation. If Clive died from a stroke, was it anything to do with their conversation? Nothing to do with me going to The Grange at all. It's bloody confusing."

"So, what are you going to do?" Lily asked gently.

"I haven't a clue. I called you because you're the only one who knows about all this. I can't talk about it to anyone else. Not yet."

"Do you want me to come?"

"Come?"

"Yes, should I come to Bath?"

"No, I don't see any reason for you to do that."

"I will if you want me to. If you want me to come with you to The Grange, if you want me to come with you when you see him again, the solicitor."

"I don't know that I can, Lily. I don't know if I can go and see him again. Knowing that he knows. I never told anybody but you. All the time I'm in his office I'll be wondering what he's thinking. And wouldn't it look a bit odd anyway? You know, no offence, but you're not family or anything, are you?"

It was a valid point so she let it go for the moment. "Perhaps he's always known, Terry. Perhaps he has always known all of it, and Clive rang him to let him know the cat was out of the bag. Do you think that's possible?"

"Oh shit. I don't know what to do. I need to think this through."

"The offer is there, Terry. If you need me, I'll come. I can stay in a hotel. I won't put you out."

"For now, let's just leave it. I'm going to The Grange in the next hour, see what the situation is there. I believe they've already taken Clive away. To the funeral director. Andrew arranged it."

She had to ask him yet again, "So, no post-mortem or anything then."

"Well, no, I guess not. But you asked that before. Do you think there should be?"

"No, no. I just wondered, that's all."

"I expect they'll tell me when I see them."

"Well don't hesitate, just let me know if I can do anything."

"I will. If I get the chance I'll give you a ring. I'm in turmoil, Lily. You would think that him being dead would solve things but it hasn't. It just hasn't, it's opened up more stuff I think. I can't just let this go, you do see that, don't you? If that old fart, Andrew Stoner, knew about Peter, if I find out he had any idea about what was happening with my mum back then, or God forbid, with me, then it's not over, is it? Even though Clive is out of it, it's not over. It's just another phase, only just begun."

Chapter 46

Lily tried to concentrate on clearing her desk. She was brutal. Old photographs that she had treasured for years were dumped into a bin bag. Letters and postcards followed them. How pointless it all seemed, this hanging onto the past and wallowing in sentiment. Her mind strayed constantly to Bath, to Terry and his struggle. It was where she wanted to be, so, she would go.

As the decision firmed in her mind she realised there may not be the opportunity. If they had suspected, if the people at the home had called the police, even now they would be searching for her and she may not go anywhere ever again. She attempted to research the issue online, how long it might take for the alarm to be raised, the police involved. What the procedure would entail.

It was confusing and did nothing except wind up the tension.

She went into the basement. For a while she sat in the candle-lit space in silence, tried to calm her rushing thoughts in the quiet, with her baby, their baby. She knew that this was just more wallowing, but what else could she do? The thought of him had ruled her life for so long and would continue to do so until she made him safe. Terry had much to decide, but then so did she, and if the police came and she had to act, to take her pills, she still had not protected Peter.

She wouldn't be able to wait much longer. Time was running out. She would have to speak to Terry. It was a failure and she would lose him, just as she had lost Peter, but she had gone so far now and she had to take it to the end.

As if the thought had caused the event, she heard her phone ringing out from where it sat on the table in the hall. It took a while to climb back to the hall but she made it before the ringing stopped.

"Lily, I hope it's not too late. You weren't in bed, were you?"

"No, I was in the basement."

"Oh right, I didn't know you had a basement. Is it habitable?"

She smiled, the property manager had quickly come to the fore. "No, it's not."

"Sorry, automatic response."

She heard him chuckle. It made her smile.

"Anyway, I'm just letting you know that I'm back from The Grange. It didn't take that long really. It was pretty much a formality. Final arrangements, just what you'd expect."

She waited, looked down at her hand and was surprised to see that she had crossed her fingers. A childish habit that had resurfaced in this moment of high tension. "Did they give you any details? You know, about the actual, erm... the end?"

"They said that he was found by the nurse when she took in his morning tea. They had looked in during the night and he'd been sleeping."

She knew that this couldn't be true. If they had checked on him properly, they would have found him dead. So, for all the quiet luxury, things were not quite as well-managed as it seemed in the upmarket care home. No matter how much you paid, no matter how smart the furnishings and decorations, at the end of the day, people were people. They would take shortcuts, particularly, she imagined, when they saw no real cause for concern.

"Are you there, Lily?"

"Yes, sorry. I'm a bit tired."

"Right, well, I'll let you go. I just thought you'd like to know."

"I'm glad you rang. Tell me about the arrangements?"

"Arrangements?" Terry sounded puzzled.

"Yes, the funeral and so on."

"Oh right. Yes. Well, Clive had it pretty much organised apparently. When the home rang Andrew Stoner, he told them who to use and that all enquiries, God knows who he thinks would be enquiring, are to be directed to him. As I said, all a formality really. But I do have some thoughts. He might not have it all his own way. But that's for later, about the grave, and it's not your problem."

She was still not reassured, so she risked the question that was nagging at her mind, "So, no post-mortem or anything?"

"No, they just called the doctor who was looking after him this morning. He certified the death as a stroke, they stressed that they had been struggling a bit with his blood pressure, and that's it. They did say that I could ask for a post-mortem myself if I wanted, apparently, they are obliged to tell me that. Did you have one, when Charlotte died?"

"No. Of course her death was expected, a relief to be honest."

"It's just that you've asked about it a couple of times and I wondered if it was something I should be thinking about. It was very straightforward with mum, her being in the hospital. I'm just letting Andrew Stoner look after it right now, to be honest. He was so pleased with himself, so smug, let him do the running around. Look, I'm keeping you up, I'm going now. I'm going to have a massive brandy and then see if I can get to sleep. God, what a day it's been."

"Alright. Good night, Terry. Sleep well."

There was no risk of the police knocking on her door, there was to be no shame, no need to take the pills to escape the authorities. She could live a while longer, help Terry. A smile crept across her face. She had literally got away with murder.

She felt energised, a little hysterical. The horror, dread and disgust had dissipated to be replaced with something that she could only describe as joy.

Chapter 47

Milsom Street in Bath city centre had been trimmed, there were multi-coloured umbrellas strung between the buildings. It was faintly ridiculous, but Lily couldn't help but smile. When she discovered it was to acknowledge the idea of Rainbow Love she felt a lump in her throat.

She had been a part of that war, hadn't she? But then, they hadn't really fought, hadn't been warriors for the cause. All that she and Charlotte Mary had done was to live their own lives in their own way. But they'd done it quietly, sneakily, if she was honest. Whenever it became uncomfortable, they had fallen back on the *Friends since school and it just made sense to pool our resources* story or even pretended to be sisters.

Looking at the rainbow flags and the bright domes floating above the street, she felt shame. Not because of their choices, but because they had been cowardly in the face of truth. Still, that had been then, it had been dangerous and the publishing, rather 'arty' world, that they had inhabited had been accepting, so the issue of their sexuality hadn't loomed as large as it could have done. And of course, Charlotte Mary had been the stronger one and she had enjoyed being on the outside of the mainstream.

There had been times, quickly pushed aside, when Lily had wondered just how much of their relationship was built on true affection, and how much was bravado and daring. On her part, she had been completely enamoured of Charlotte Mary, but there had always been an element of fear. She knew that her partner could be shallow and insincere and there had been a low-grade but constant worry that she would become bored and decide to try something new. She flirted with men and really it was hard to believe that she had ever felt anything deeply. Bisexual probably, and simply out to enjoy any and all experiences that were available to her. How Lily wished she had been so daring.

What would Charlotte Mary have made of Lily's new secret? She nodded to herself, she would probably have been excited by it. She would have thought it the greatest thrill. At last, Lily would have impressed her.

She was old, it was too late now for her to make any difference to things that had happened in the past, or indeed, the young people that she saw around her. There was no point in pretending. When they looked at her they wouldn't even consider her sexuality. She was a rather dowdy, unimportant woman. They didn't know her truth, and now she had a second one, a greater one: as she moved along with the crowd she felt isolated, but also, she was amazed to find, she felt special and superior. It was an unfamiliar sensation.

* * *

Terry waved at her through the window of the tea shop. He looked tired, there were dark rings under his eyes and two tiny grooves between his eyebrows that she had never noticed before.

"I was surprised when you rang me, you didn't need to come, Lily. I don't like to put you out like this. To be honest I don't know what you can do."

Of course he didn't know how much she had already been able to do. "I thought I might be able to help. You'll

193

have a lot to do and it'll help if you have someone to talk to. I wasn't doing anything else, and I kept thinking about you."

"That's good of you, thanks. Really, thanks, but…" He pursed his lips and glanced around, awkward and ill at ease. "Thing is that, well, maybe I can just get through it quicker if I just zoom around, you know, on my own. I have to keep things ticking over with the business, there are meetings and what have you. Stoner is taking care of funeral arrangements right now, there's not much to do on that front. Honestly, Lily, it's kind of you but, well, really there's no need."

She smiled at him. "Yes, you're probably right but I like Bath and I'm just rattling round at home, I enjoy the train journey, and you were on my mind."

He leaned across and squeezed her hand. "You've been ever so good, Lily, I do appreciate it. When things have settled down a bit, when things are clearer in my own mind, I'll come through to Southsea. We'll get those ashes and then bring them back, and we'll have some sort of little thing, a ceremony, and put Peter with his mum. I know that's what you wanted. I know that's why you came in the first place. Is that okay? Shall we do that?"

"Yes, let's do that. It'll be good to have that sorted."

"Actually, that's something I'm dealing with today. No way is Clive going into the grave with Mum and Gran, I'm just not having it, so I'm arranging for a cremation somewhere else. Stoner's trying to interfere but I'm determined about this. So, there we are, Peter can go with them, in the family plot."

"And what about all the other things? What about the abuse, the baby selling, all of that?"

He shook his head and sighed deeply. "I don't know. I just don't know any more. It's too late, isn't it? Clive's dead, there's no way to make him pay, not really, and to be honest, I don't know that I've got the heart for it. When you said yesterday that maybe Andrew Stoner had known about it…" He paused. "Well, it made me see how embarrassing all this will be if I pursue it and really, is there any point anymore?"

"It's got to be your decision, of course, Terry, but it seems a shame. What about the others, and what about Peter?"

He looked at her, a question in his eyes. "How much difference can it really make, do you think? I'll be honest, this has thrown me off-balance a bit, Clive dying right now. I've thought about it all night, and really, if he did die because of me showing him that report, and telling him that I knew all about his dirty secrets, well, do you see? That is a sort of revenge. In a way, he has paid. So, I can live with that. I can happily live with that. It wasn't deliberate, not as if I even hoped for it to happen – but…" He nodded and shrugged. "It's a way out and it feels like a sort of victory."

She was disappointed, but couldn't force Terry to act if he had decided against it. In a way, she had already had the ultimate revenge, but that was to be her secret and it really wasn't enough. It had become a dignified escape for the person who had caused all this and no justice for the others. She struggled to hold down the anger, it was not against Terry, he was damaged and in some ways fragile, but she wasn't yet satisfied, it still wasn't over for her.

She tried a different tack. "What about the solicitor though. He probably knows everything now. Aren't you going to do anything about that? Surely you should try and find out. If he knew he should pay as well, shouldn't he? What about the other people, have you given up on the thought of doing something for them?"

"I told you already, I'm not some sort of crusader, Lily. Clive's dead – I don't know if this can go any further. Anyway, at the moment I can only take things a step at a time I think."

"So, it's almost over for you?"

"I think it is, yes. I will always be grateful that you made me act. I do feel better, I feel as though facing him has sort of drawn a line under it. You coming and wanting to set Mum's mind at rest has led to this, so I owe you, Lily. Listen, I'll tell you what. Since you're here anyway why don't you stay tonight, we'll go out and have a meal? We'll sort out what to do about Peter and then tomorrow, if I can fit it in, I'll give you a lift back to Southsea. Could you do that, do you think? I'll help you find a hotel if you like."

She nodded at him. "That would be lovely. Don't worry about me finding somewhere to stay, I know where I can go."

Chapter 48

It was strange being back in the hotel. Lily had thought she would never see it again but so much had changed. She was stronger now, she had done something that most people would never dream of. And she had got away with it. Of course, she had done it because of Terry, and Peter, but mostly Terry. It had been a duty.

There was no regret. There had been dreadful fear, and shock, but not any regret. Even when she allowed the memory to trickle in – the final moments, that strange last breath, the terrible aftermath – from just this couple of days' distance, she felt strong and powerful. She hadn't enjoyed doing it, but it had been necessary and it was done.

She couldn't waste time dwelling on what had happened. There was still more work needed.

Terry didn't know that she had already booked into the hotel and brought clothes with her; that she had never intended to go straight home. Not with so much unfinished business.

She took a hot shower and dressed in her black dress. It would be fine if he didn't have time to take her back tomorrow. She had brought plenty of clothes and anyway,

Bath was full of lovely shops. It would be an ideal time to spend some of the money that had been sitting in her account for an age. It would be fun, and she found she was open to the idea of a grand final flourish before the end.

She took her medication and made sure the spray was in her bag. She felt better than she had for a while. Having something to do, someone else to think about apart from herself, was good. She pulled the chair in front of the window and gazed out at the view over the little pond and the busy road beyond.

The afternoon wore on and she took a nap. Seven o'clock came, and she began to worry. There was nothing on the phone's missed call list. It was so tempting to ring, to pretend to have forgotten whether they had already arranged something. Anxiety built; perhaps there really had been a misunderstanding. She replayed the conversation in her head and was convinced that he had told her he would ring. There was nothing else to do but wait.

It was after half past seven when the call came. "Lily, I'm sorry. I meant to ring earlier. Something's come up. I'll pick you up in about ten minutes if that's alright. Do you think you could manage a little walk? There are a couple of pubs just near to where you are, they are both very nice. If that suits, I'll call and book a table."

"Lovely. I'm feeling fine, Terry, you really mustn't worry about me so much, truly."

Immediately after they met, Lily knew that there was something very wrong. He offered her his arm, but there was no smile, and the short walk to the pub was silent. "What would you like to drink, Lily?"

"A glass of red wine please, something heavy."

He smiled as she repeated the words from their first meeting.

They ordered and she took her first sip of the Bordeaux. "Oh lovely, that's perfect, thank you."

He responded with a short nod and drank half of his pint of lager in a couple of deep gulps. It was a replay of the first time, and even the atmosphere was a mirror: he was distracted and edgy; he let out a huge sigh.

She could wait no longer. "What's the matter?"

He shook his head, but then lifted his eyes to look directly across the table at her. "I had a meeting earlier, with Andrew Stoner. That's what kept me. It was supposed to be a short thing. Just to talk about the funeral, but it took longer than expected. That's why I was late."

Lily took a sip of her drink. Her hands shook, but he didn't seem to notice. "Was there something wrong?"

"Yes, you could say that."

She was afraid to speak, afraid of his next words.

"So, Clive." He paused again, he was struggling to format what he wanted to tell her.

"Yes?" She kept her voice calm but her stomach was churning. Here it comes she thought, they've found out.

"He's screwed me. Even from beyond the bloody grave. Well, not in the grave yet, but you know what I mean. Even though he's dead, he's screwed me over. Sorry for the language, Lily, but I am so bloody mad."

This wasn't what she had been expecting. She would have felt relief if it hadn't been for the furious fire in Terry's eyes, the way he picked up the drink, drained the glass and slammed it back on the table.

"What on earth has happened, Terry? Tell me, what's happened?"

"I'm sorry, Lily, this isn't your concern. Look, let's just have our meal and talk about something else."

"Well, I came here to help you, Terry. If you need to talk about something, get something off your chest, then I don't mind you using me. I'd like it."

He gave her an odd look, but then he tried to smile. It was a poor effort, just an upward movement of his lips but it was enough to let her know that he wasn't angry with her.

"Okay, well, you know I always said that I reckoned it would all be mine one day? The properties, the business? I stuck with it, worked for him, even though I despised him, because I told myself I was really working for myself, my future?"

Lily nodded, and she whispered a response, "Is this about the will?"

"It is."

"Has he not left it to you then? Oh, Terry!"

He shook his head as he answered, "It's not quite that bad. Although in a way it's worse. He's left it to me, most of it anyway. There are a couple of places that he has left to friends, their own homes and I guess that's fair enough. A bit over-generous in a way but…" He shrugged his shoulders.

"But…?" Lily asked.

As they ate he explained about the meeting. How Andrew Stoner had gloated as he had relayed the terms of Terry's inheritance. How for the next ten years he, the solicitor, would manage a trust that would dictate most of how the business was run.

"But it's still yours?" Lily was confused by the terms he was using.

"Yes, in name it's mine. I'll still have the day-to-day running. The donkey work. Dealing with agents, contractors, all of that. But nothing else. None of the ongoing expansion or development of the business. None of the stuff that he, Clive, used to do. For the next ten years, anything at all to do with that will have to be approved by Andrew bloody Stoner. Even my own flat. If I want to sell that I'll have to go to him. It wouldn't have mattered if we'd been on the same page about this stuff, but he's like Clive was. Stuck in the mud, ticking along. He just wants things to stay the way they've always been. No expansion, no new investment – oh, all sorts of ideas I had. Stuff I've tried to get Clive to do for years. Now… now the old bugger is dead, I still have to wait. Another ten bloody years before I have control. It's so unfair, Lily. I'll be too old by then to do what I want. You have to get this stuff going as soon as you can, build up your money, organise pensions. I just feel like giving up, I just feel like throwing in the towel."

"Is that why Clive made that call then, after we'd been to see him, is that why he called the solicitor?"

"No. God, no – ha – if only. If it had been, then there was no way they would have time to make it legal. No, this is something they cooked up between themselves ages ago. When Clive started to get better from his stroke. I guess he'd had a glimpse of his own mortality. I was trying to get him to sign things over and, well it just backfired, didn't it? He wanted to make sure that, even if he wasn't here, he was still controlling things. The old swine."

"But, Terry, you can't give up, what would you do then?"

"I'd just go. I've thought about it before, when things have been getting me down. I'd just leave the whole bloody lot and emigrate. Go to America maybe, Australia, somewhere I could make a new start and leave all of this stuff behind."

"Oh, that would be a terrible shame. Why should you have to do that?"

In response, he shrugged his shoulders huffily.

"Well, what I mean is, you shouldn't let him win. It's your right, he owes you. You know that. More than an ordinary grandfather, father – he owes you, Terry. It's awful to think that he could still win. He mustn't."

He smiled at her, it was warmer than before. It seemed that her words had helped. "Oh look, Lily. This isn't your problem. Don't let it upset you. I need to think about it all and see what my options are. But quite honestly, right now, I just feel as though I want done with it all."

"He's old, Andrew Stoner, isn't he?"

"Same age as Clive was, yes."

"Well there we are. Maybe he won't live another ten years. What happens if he dies?"

"Oh well, I'm not a hundred percent certain, but I'm pretty sure that in that case I get complete control. There were no other conditions, no-one else mentioned. Ha, that's the answer, perhaps I should push him under a bus or something, eh?"

Chapter 49

Lily was angry. She was furious with Clive. How could he have done this selfish thing to his own son? After everything else, it was a final vicious act that had stolen from Terry the promise of being his own master. It was what had given him hope for a better future. She was livid with Andrew Stoner for going along with it, and selfishly, she was angry that they had spoiled her evening with Terry. In the face of the rest of it this was a minor thing, but the fury was all-encompassing.

Terry had told her not to worry, that he would be working out the best way to deal with it and that, if it was at all possible, he would find a way to change it. He had been preoccupied and edgy, and the evening was a bit of a damp squib; so, it seemed that even now Clive was influencing their lives.

When he had spoken to her about the journey back to Hampshire the next day, she had told him no. She wouldn't hear of him spending time running her back and forth when there was so much more important work for him to do. There was no denying the look of relief on his face.

It was tempting to stay here, in Bath, but she had work of her own to do. She must change her will; Charlotte Mary's nephew was no longer the right option. She would leave him something, a small bequest out of respect for his past kindness. It was obvious that everything else must be left for Terry. After all, he was Peter's brother, and the closest thing that she would ever have to a son.

After their meal, he had walked with her to the hotel, seen her safely inside and promised to ring her the next day if there were any major developments.

"I wonder about coming to his funeral?"

"Clive's?" Terry had frowned. "Why would you want to do that?"

"Support, you need support at that sort of thing."

"No, really there's no need. I've got a couple of mates who have already said they'll come. Not because they liked him or anything but, well yes, as you say just so there's somebody there for me. But it's alright, I've got it covered. I don't know yet how many people there'll be. He had all his cronies, his Lodge brothers and what not, but I'm leaving it all to Stoner. It's a kind thought but it's not worth it. I'm not intending to go to the gathering afterwards, I'll get out of that. I'm not spending time with that crowd. Thanks though."

However, Lily was still determined to go, to see the final act. She'd let him know when she was already there. She had the name of the funeral directors. It would be easy to find out the day and time of the ceremony.

She watched him walk through the carpark towards the river. Soon she expected that he was going to ask again about Peter, and she had to decide how to handle that. She could go along with the pretence, let him put Charlotte Mary's ashes with Carol Robertson, believing they were Peter's remains, and then there would be nothing left to say. He would go back to his own life and she would be left alone with everything still unresolved – Peter still in the cold cellar. She would have failed.

It was hard to sleep. Here was a whole new set of problems. She remembered the night at The Grange, it caused her stomach to turn. Andrew Stoner was no weak, old victim, but a man who was doubtless stronger than she, with all his faculties. She had already proved that she was capable of things far beyond anything imaginable, but that wasn't an option this time. For this situation, she needed a new idea. A different tack.

One way or another, the blight of Andrew Stoner must be removed from Terry's future.

She gathered together thoughts of what she knew and let the ideas play out in her mind. The two men had been friends for a long time and Clive had called Stoner the day before his death. The old solicitor must know about the past. If he knew about Terry, about the other baby, her Peter, then what else was he aware of?

In recent cases of child abuse, the nets had been cast wide and drawn in unimaginable numbers of criminals. Could it be that both Stoner and Clive Robertson had been involved in the filthy business with a circle of others? Why had he left expensive property to friends? Even the kindest, most altruistic person would think twice about such bequests, especially if they formed part of a greater whole.

She became convinced that Clive had been involved in the worst of all cruelty, not only with his own family but others besides. It seemed to her more than likely that he had not acted alone and Andrew Stoner could be the thin edge of a much greater wedge. She had never imagined that she would be involved in this dirty business, but acknowledged that in a way Peter had brought her to this, and she was not going to let him down again.

As the road outside began to stir with the earliest of the traffic and the sun sent a gentle glow into the mists cloaking the hills around the city, Lily rolled over and fell asleep.

The next morning, she phoned to arrange an appointment with the solicitor.

The answering machine promised that they would get back to her as soon as possible, assured her that she was important to them. She left a message, a little arrogant, rather pre-emptive. She told them she would be back in Bath on Monday afternoon and her time was limited. She wanted to deal only with Andrew Stoner. He had been recommended to her, and she was considering instructing him to deal with her recently deceased partner's extensive holdings.

She left them her address and mobile number. She must be convincing, and if they were moved to check the few facts, she had said nothing untrue.

She considered waiting out the weekend in the hotel, but if she were to bump into Terry it would be very difficult to explain and she couldn't sit in the room for two days. In any case, there was work for her to do in Southsea.

Before she left, she walked into town. She bought a new outfit, something exclusive, something more like the sort of thing Charlotte Mary would have had, and she added some new shoes – the first for years. It was all a part of the plan which was becoming ever clearer in her mind.

* * *

Lily went home, rested and waited for Monday. She wrote her letter, organised the train ticket, and sorted through Charlotte Mary's jewellery. The large Sapphire ring was a little gaudy for daywear, but it was a statement piece and she would also wear the earrings. She dressed in her new outfit, gazed at herself in the mirror and was satisfied.

She had lost a little weight and looked even older than her age now, but her thinner figure was smarter. She had become a pastiche of her mother and Charlotte Mary. Of the dumpy, frowsy Lily of more recent years, there was little trace. It made her smile. In the back of the wardrobe was a walking stick. It was one that her father had carried, dark shiny wood and a silver handle. It was a little long for her but manageable. It was the finishing touch. Yes, a dowager with a stick and rather more money than she needed. A new Lily.

Chapter 50

The call from the solicitors came while Lily was on the train. The appointment they offered was in the early afternoon. Her nerves were jumping, but she managed to keep her voice firm and controlled.

Apart from one pass along the street where the offices were located, she kept away. The character that she was about to play wouldn't wander back and forth. She would turn up in time for her appointment, and so she did.

She was offered coffee by a secretary behind a workstation in the dull waiting room that she declined with a small smile.

As she entered his office leaning heavily on the cane, Andrew Stoner walked out from behind the desk to hold the chair. She took her seat, placing her bag and the small document case on the floor beside her.

"Have you been offered coffee, tea?"

"I was, thank you, and I think that now maybe a cup of tea would be nice."

He pressed a button on his intercom, ordered two cups of tea.

"So, Mrs, erm… Bowers? I believe our name was passed along to you?"

"It's Miss, Miss Lily Bowers. Yes, indeed. I heard about you, specifically you, in dealings with Clive Robertson. I believe he is a friend?"

The shock on the solicitor's face was quickly hidden and he managed a question, "Did you know him well?"

"Not terribly well, no. Actually, it was my partner who had dealings with him."

"Ah. Well, I'm afraid Clive is no longer with us."

She lowered her brow, tipped her head. "I knew that he was ill."

Stoner coughed. "I'm afraid Mr Robertson, Clive, died last week. It was quite sudden. He did seem to be improving, but then…" Stoner shrugged. "I suppose these things happen. It was a shock. We had been friends for a long time." He had taken out his handkerchief to blow his nose. She was surprised to see such visible grief.

"So, you were close?"

The solicitor nodded, and then turned as his assistant knocked and carried a tray into the room. There was a hiatus while cups were moved, sugar and biscuits offered, napkins passed, by which time Andrew Stoner had regained his composure. "So, your own partner has recently passed?"

In response, Lily simply inclined her head.

"You weren't married?"

"No. We never felt the need."

"And from what I understand, he had various holdings that you have inherited."

"She."

"I'm sorry?"

"My partner's name was Charlotte Mary Stone."

"Ah I see, a business partner." He smiled and lifted his cup to cover his moment of confusion.

"No, indeed." Lily was enjoying this little back and forth. She watched silently as he re-gathered his thoughts and struggled to find a suitable expression.

"I am sorry for your loss."

She had to bite back a smile as he reverted to the overused phrase. Again, she rewarded him with a small nod, and allowed a sigh.

He obviously decided that the best idea was to move on with the business at hand.

"How do you think we will be able to help you? We offer investment advice, property management services, will-writing services, of course. Erm…"

Lily bent and lifted the document case onto her lap. She slid her hand inside and pulled out the small brown paper bag.

"My reason for coming to see you is possibly quite unusual. Some years ago, my partner made a purchase. I suppose it would be true to call it an investment."

Andrew Stoner was frowning. He peered across his desk at the scruffy little bag in her hand, and then raised his eyes to hers. He had no idea the way this was going, but she imagined he was wondering if this was all a waste of his time.

Lily leaned forward and tipped the contents of the bag onto the leather blotter.

Stoner glanced at her, frowned. "I'm sorry, I don't understand. What are these?" He poked at the sad little collection of items.

Lily half stood and picked up the flimsy blue card. She turned it in her hand until the writing was visible on the top, picked up the receipt, then placed the two together into his outstretched hand.

She knew immediately that she had him. It was clear by the way his colour changed, leaving him grey and drawn. He glanced across at her. Grunted, and then discarded the papers with a flick. "What on earth is this? What are these things? I am not sure I understand exactly what is going on here, Miss Bowers. How can I help you with… with these?" He pointed at the desktop and Lily was delighted by the quiver in the blunt-ended fingers.

He was panicked and falling apart in front of her eyes. It was better than she could have hoped for. Her nerves settled and she felt confidence flood her body. "Well, now. I can tell you exactly how you can help me. As for what's going on, I think you know only too well."

Chapter 51

"I see from your face, from your eyes, that you know just what these mean." As she gathered the papers and baby bracelet, and replaced them in the paper bag, Lily spoke softly. Inside, her heart thundered, she felt the burn in her throat, but she had to control it. If she was forced to take out the medical spray, she would lose the upper hand.

She took a moment, covered the pause by taking another sip of tea. She managed a cold smile when she raised her head, and looked back at him, across his great desk.

"Charlotte Mary conspired with Clive Robertson. Between them they conceived a dreadful deal. It was illegal certainly, and it was also immoral and desperately cruel. You know this, of course. Your friend was a terrible person, as are you, Mr Stoner. You and others. I'll be honest, I don't know the names of all of them, not yet, but no matter, that won't be my responsibility. What I do know is that terrible evil was conducted between you all. Under cover of respectability. Using power and privilege, threats and bullying, you stole lives and ruined futures."

She was guessing most of it, putting together a situation that was mostly imagination, and she was painfully aware that she mustn't go too far. While he sat silently gaping at her across the expanse of polished wood, she assumed that she was not far from the truth. She must stop before she gave herself away. She waved a hand in the air. "Oh, you know already, I won't sully my mouth with it all. Except to say that I am ready and very willing to turn everything I know, everything I have, over to the police."

"So, why haven't you?" He was recovering, slowly, and he spoke carefully. She had to hold the advantage.

"Because, in spite of the wicked thing she did, I loved my partner. But now she's dead and it can't hurt her. She has no family left to speak of, no-one to worry about her reputation, so here we are. But there is more."

He didn't speak. She waited, gave him a chance to ask the question, and when he didn't, she was forced to carry on. She touched the brown bag, slid it a little way across the desk.

"This child. This sweet little boy had a brother. Ah, I see you know just who I mean. Tracing our son's family..." She wanted him to believe that Peter was still alive, that she could present to the world a young man who had been treated as a commodity. She went on, "I have come to know Terry. He is a fine young person. I know I don't have to tell you the struggles he has had, the terrible things that he has overcome. I have become very fond of him. And now, I find that you and his, well, his what? What shall we call him? I think we'll stick to Clive, because the other titles are too good for him. Yes, Clive. Between you, you have concocted an arrangement that will rob him of even more than he has lost already."

"It's none of your business. My legal dealings with clients have nothing to do with you," Stoner said.

She saw the colour creep back into his face, painted there by rising fury.

"If you have all this proof, this knowledge, then why haven't you taken any action?"

Lily shook her head, just once, and she tutted with a click of her tongue. "I told you, I waited until Charlotte was safe. But you need to know that I have taken action. I have left a letter with my solicitor. At the moment, he is simply holding it for me. But should I call him, then he has instructions to take it to the authorities."

"Why are you here? Why you, why not the police? I'm not sure I believe you, Miss Bowers," he spat her name at her. He was stronger by the minute. Used to dealing with underlings, with frightened, desperate people, used to being in charge. He was regaining his nerve.

"I am here to give you an opportunity to save yourself from what's coming. It would be hard for all of us, not only the despicable creatures involved, but the innocents as well. We would all suffer. I want to help Terry. I want to make his life easier, to give him hope of a better future and if to do that I have to show you a way out, then I'm willing to make that sacrifice. He is my son's brother after all, I have come to regard him affectionately, as my own boy, and you know mothers – mothers make sacrifices for their children.

"Now, either you can carry out Clive Robertson's instructions, and sit in your fine office while the whole weight of the law and public opinion crush you." She paused, caught her breath. "Or, you can retire. You can sign over the whole of the Robertson business to Terry, give him what is, after all, his birth right, and I will leave the letter where it is. I will take my knowledge, my evidence. I will take all of it with me to the grave. And for the avoidance of doubt, I do have more than this." She indicated the baby things. "There is DNA evidence which, as you will know, is irrefutable." She watched as he sank. She knew now for certain what Clive Robertson had told him during the final phone call, so, inadvertently, the old man had been instrumental in her success.

He pointed at her. "You, you're the woman who went with Terry to the nursing home. He said that some old crone had been there. This... this is blackmail."

All she needed to do was to nod.

He spoke again, "How do I know you'll do what you say? How do I know that you'll keep your word? How do I know Terry won't say something? How do I know that I can trust either of you? He bullied his grandfather." He stopped as Lily raised her eyes. "He was a sick man, very distressed when he called me. How do I know that I can trust anything that either of you say?"

"You don't. Though he is rather keener than I am to avoid the furore. He finds the whole thing too painful. Why do you imagine he hasn't spoken out yet, after all? And why would he now when things are beginning to improve for him? If he had a business to run, he would want to direct attention away from the nastier side of his history. Now that Clive is dead, he would prefer to simply get on with his life. Because of that, you won't tell him I've been here. I don't want to ruin our new and rather fragile relationship with this nastiness. I can help him through it if I need to, but I would prefer to see him happy and successful on his own terms."

She slid to the front of the chair, bent and picked up her bags. Using the walking stick, which she was glad of now, she stood on her shaking legs, straightened her spine and before she turned to leave she spoke again, firm but quiet. "What you must know is this, if I don't hear within the next two days that you have done as I ask, then the letter will go to the police, along with this." She wagged the document carrier at him. "And you will be in... oh, now, what is that wonderful modern expression? Ah yes, you'll be in a 'world of hurt'." She managed a small chuckle as she left him, red-faced and anxious behind the antique desk.

Chapter 52

Lily held herself together long enough to stalk through the front office and out into the road. Once around the corner she stopped and leaned against the pale stone wall. She pulled out her nitroglycerin spray and closed her eyes as she waited for the medication to take effect.

She could hear the buzz of traffic and the clomp of feet around her. The rumble of conversation, punctuated by shouts and squeals, faded into the distance and she felt herself begin to drift away.

"Are you alright, love?" There was the sudden weight of a hand on her arm, bringing her back. She opened her eyes to stare into the sun-wrinkled face peeking out from under a yellow hard hat.

He spoke again, "Are you okay, only you look a bit shook up? I saw you with your little inhaler thing." He pointed down towards her hand which still gripped the spray bottle.

He cupped her elbow with his big, calloused hand, the rough skin of his fingers clicked on the fine fabric of her suit. He was steady and strong and she leaned on him as he helped her to one of the benches in the middle of the precinct.

"Now, do you want me to get you an ambulance?" He pulled out his mobile phone.

Lily shook her head. "No, there's no need. I'll be fine in a minute. Thank you so much."

He smiled and plonked down on the seat beside her.

"You gave me a bit of a start then. I thought you were going to slide down that wall and land on the flags." He laughed and she found herself smiling in response.

"Oh, it's a nuisance, it's just a silly condition. I'm not supposed to get het up."

"Right, and have you?"

"Yes, I'm afraid I have. I've just been talking to a solicitor and it was quite – upsetting."

"Ha, them blokes yes, well, I can imagine. But there, your colour's coming back now. Are you feeling better?"

"I am, thank you, yes. I wonder, would you mind awfully just giving me a hand over to that little café? I think if I have a nice cup of tea, I'm sure I'll be fine."

"Come on, my lover." He held out his thick arm and she leaned against him as they walked across the pavement. He pushed open the door, and ushered her inside.

"Thank you so much, you've been very kind."

He gave her a final smile, a rather cheeky wink and admonished, "You take care now," and he was gone, out through the door and into the crowd.

* * *

Journeys often seem shorter the more they are taken, but today it seemed that she would never reach home. The confrontation had taken far more out of her than she could ever have imagined it would, and she had no way of knowing what the eventual outcome would be.

She sat in an unhappy huddle on the train and dragged herself miserably through the Southsea streets as dusk fell. The rooms were chilly, she poured a large whisky and crawled up to the bedroom. She stripped off the new clothes which felt grubby and uncomfortable, and wrapped herself in a thick woollen dressing gown.

Replaying the events in her mind, at first she was filled with pride. She had faced the monster and she had seen him crumble. There was still the chance that he would ignore her, take the risk that she was bluffing. It was possible he wouldn't change his life, give up his career and run away. But she had tried, she had done all that she could and though there was nothing more that she could think of, she had given everything she could to help Terry.

It was hard to rest after the stress of the long day, and the morning found her sick and exhausted.

She spent hours dosing fitfully in the chair in front of the fire. She knew she should call the doctor but couldn't summon the energy. Eventually, mid-way through the afternoon, she managed to calm the clamour in her brain; she closed her eyes and gave herself up to whatever would come.

* * *

The ringing of her phone from the bottom of her bag roused her with a start.

"Lily. Hello. It's Terry."

"Hello."

"Are you okay?"

She struggled to straighten in the chair and collect her addled wits. "Yes, I'm fine. I was having a nap."

"Oh shit, sorry. I'll ring later."

"No, it's fine, really. I'm awake now and it's time I erm…" The sentence fizzled because she couldn't think of what she really wanted or needed to do.

"Are you sure? Only, to be honest I was pretty excited, and I just wanted to talk to someone. You're the only one who knows about it all. So, I rang you." She glanced at the clock, it was after five in the evening, the day had drifted past.

"Yes. I'm wide awake now. What's happened?"

"Well, I don't think I really know myself, to be honest. I'm still trying to process it, trying to get my thoughts in order."

Chapter 53

As Terry gabbled at her in excitement, she was at first disbelieving, and then exultant. When the chatter from the other end quieted for a few seconds, she managed to ask, "So, let me be sure I understand you. Andrew Stoner has retired?"

"That's what they told me. Through the girl I spoke to, well, woman I suppose – anyway, one of the junior partners." He was still falling over his words with the thrill of what had happened and Lily grinned as she tried to make sense of it.

"She said that it had been a sudden decision, brought on, she thought, by the death of a close friend. Well we know who that is, don't we? Anyway, he just said that he didn't want to die at his desk and he was finishing. She called it unprofessional, and then corrected herself saying that there may be other reasons, such as ill health, that he didn't want to reveal. She said they were in turmoil and trying to reach his clients and handle the outstanding issues as quickly as possible. Anyway, the upshot of all of it is, there is no-one else to take on the stuff in Clive's will to do with my company."

Lily smiled, already it was 'his' company.

He was still speaking, "It was so very specific, the will I mean, naming him, and precluding anyone else in the practice. I reckon that was so that if he had died, like you said might happen, nobody else could be running Clive's business. He wouldn't have wanted that. He wanted it to be bloody Stoner and if it wasn't him, then it wouldn't be the same – it wouldn't make the point to me that he was trying to get across: that even though he's dead, he's in charge. Well he's not – I've won Lily, I've bloody won! She was apologetic, can you believe it, she actually said that they were sorry. I don't know how I managed to keep quiet. It's brilliant. I wonder what's wrong with him? I hope it's something terrible. I know that's probably not what I'm supposed to say, but the old sod deserves it." At last he fell silent.

"Well it's all a bit sudden, isn't it, and wonderful of course. I am so pleased for you, I really am."

When he spoke again he was quieter, "There is just one thing though. I know I said I'd come through and deal with those ashes, take you to bury them. Thing is, I think the next couple of weeks are going to be a bit frantic for me. I've got the funeral and then there's a lot of meetings, plus the usual stuff with the business and sorting out Clive's other stuff. I'm getting rid of everything. I did think of having people in to do it, but, to be honest, I dread to think what they might find. I'm probably being over cautious but, well, I reckon you know what I'm talking about."

"So, what about all that? Is it over for you now, Terry? Are you letting it all go?"

"To be honest, I don't know. It'll never be over, not for me, but I'm coping with it. Never had much choice, did I? It's a bit cowardly maybe, and a bit self-centred but I don't think I'm going to do anything, for the time being at least. I'm keeping the company name and I don't want to draw attention to anything like that. If those days, when I was left in the car, really were about him forcing himself on tenants or even on their kids, or God knows what else, I don't want to poke the wasps' nest. I'm still trying to decide. I'm worried that it's just opening a can of worms and I don't think I can face it. Things have started to go really well for me at long last, and I don't want to rock the boat."

She couldn't help asking, "Do you think it's possible that Stoner had anything to do with any of that? I mean, you said you thought Clive might have been forcing other people to have sex with him. Do you really think he was acting alone? I'm thinking about all the cases you hear about, read about, they seem to be groups and gangs, don't they?"

"I know what you're getting at, Lily. I have thought about it and what I will say is that, if ever what I know will help anyone else, then I will use it. Do you think that's enough, or am I only thinking of myself?"

"At the end of the day all you can do is look after yourself, Terry. You just do that for now. I know that if anything else happens you'll see what the right thing is and you'll do it."

"That's a really nice thing to say. Look, I'm going to have to go, I'm meeting some mates. So, can we just leave it? I'll give you a call, once things calm down a bit. We'll arrange about the ashes. Be a couple of weeks I reckon. Is that okay?"

"You will keep in touch won't you, Terry?"

"Yes, of course. But, well, I'm still in a bit of a tizz."

Lily turned off the phone and laid it gently on the table. She was heartsore, it had become more and more obvious as the conversation had progressed: apart from the business with Peter's ashes there was nothing more to keep them together. He would move on and make a success of his business, and the odd lesbian woman who lived in Southsea would never cross his mind. Not until she died – and she smiled to think of his surprise when he found out he had an inheritance from her. It was cold comfort.

She felt the tickle of tears across her face. She wiped them away, it was an ending and she was bereaved. It was a happy ending though, and she must just be glad of that.

So, the end was coming, just one more meeting when they visited his mother's grave and then it would be done. There was another opportunity to see him now with all the worry gone; in charge of his own destiny. It would be a fine thing and there was nothing to stop her. Clive's funeral was a public affair, and she had already told him that she was thinking of going. It wouldn't seem so very strange, would it?

For a moment, she baulked at the idea, in the films and books she had read, the murderer often went to the victim's funeral; didn't the police hover at the edges of the group, noting who was there? And then she realised: it didn't apply. She had, after all, got away with murder.

Chapter 54

The chapel was surprisingly full, Lily had become used to the funerals of her friends, her parents' friends. Just a few bent old people sitting apart from each other in the front pews, or in wheelchairs in the aisles. Here there was quite a turnout, mostly men. There were few women, and the ones who had come obviously made one part of a couple.

Lily looked around for Terry. She couldn't find him and wondered if in the end he had made a final rebellion. She stepped forward to find a seat near the back, and that was when she saw him. He had been hidden behind a pillar nearer to the waiting bier. He stepped across the front of the place to join a small group of young men seated in the first row of seats. As he lowered to the chair, the boy next to him reached out and laid a hand on his shoulder. Terry turned and smiled at him. She didn't know how much his peers were aware of the troubles in his past, these young friends. Probably not at all, he had always insisted she was the only one who knew. So, they quite likely assumed he was mourning his grandfather, after all that was normal, natural. She saw him smile, he leaned a little towards the other young man and spoke quietly in his ear.

She had, for the first time, a genuine glimpse of the life he had made. She hadn't given it a lot of thought but saw that, though it must be based on half-truths and hidden torment, he had built it himself. He had searched out a normality that his grandfather had been hellbent on denying him. She was happy that he had a chance to make it just what he had always wanted, what he deserved. It pleased her that she had helped towards that end, but at what cost? Her heart thudded painfully as she thought of the events that had brought them to this place.

She would never be able to tell him and one of the reasons was, in the end, he wasn't hers, he never had been. He had been Carol's for a while but that poor broken girl hadn't been able to protect him. What he was now, whole and strong with just the thread of damage running through him, a fault in the rock, he had done for himself. He had fought back and struggled on.

If she tried to become more to him than she was, then she would be a leech. She had lost the baby that hadn't ever been hers to have anyway, she could not, must not, blight yet another life.

If Andrew Stoner decided to make trouble, or if he had alerted any of the others that she believed were involved in the filth of their past, then it could even now backfire and bring down trouble on them both.

Apart from all of that, and more importantly, there was what she had done at The Grange. It would ruin any relationship they might have. Despite all her efforts to put away the memory, that act was a part of her, followed her constantly, waiting until she let down her guard. She tried not to think of it, but at night, as she drifted into her uneasy sleep, the feel of Clive's dying body, tense and threshing against her, would ghost into her consciousness to torment her. How could she spend time with Terry when there would be the spectre of his father, forever between them?

She would not be a part of his life. She would keep the things secret that he didn't need to know. It surely could not harm him if it did not exist for him. The person who had stolen his childhood, and tried to control the best years of his adulthood, was gone. It was done.

She turned and tiptoed quietly towards the door. She was forced to stand aside as the attendants pushed the wheeled trolley bearing the coffin through the big doors. Music began and many of the mourners turned as she left. She was aware that he had seen her; he raised his hand, took a step forward. She shook her head and walked away. By the time she had reached the road, she was breathless and in pain, but she didn't slow, she didn't look back.

She called for a taxi to take her back to the station. As the driver wove through the endless traffic heading for the city centre and they passed the end of Lyncombe Hill, she glanced up the steep slope towards the turn into Southcote Place, and knew with absolute certainty that she would never see this place again.

There was a short wait on the draughty platform. She felt empty of emotion. The only thing left now was to get back to Peter. What a difficult journey it had been. She had not expected to be struggling still with all of this, and it was even now, unfinished business.

Her physical strength was desperately depleted and without the buzz of adrenaline to push her on, she was exhausted. She felt the end coming, unmistakably, and she felt that she must get back to her home.

The sky was darkening by the time she slipped her key into the lock and stepped into the hallway of the house in Southsea. Her limbs were heavy, and though she had used the spray, her chest was locked in a steel band. It was difficult to breathe, shadows lurked at the edges of her vision. She was afraid. Though she had known that this was coming and had wished for it and waited for it, now that it was time she was afraid. She wanted to go up to the bathroom and fetch the pills. She wanted to control this, but didn't have the energy to climb the stairs.

She picked up her flashlight and, gasping and groaning quietly as the pain intensified, she half fell, clutching at the old wooden banister, down the narrow wooden steps into the basement.

She sat on the chair, but it was too difficult to be upright, so she lowered to the hard floor. She propped her back against the damp, mouldy wall, turned the flashlight beam to where the baby slept and waited for the end.

Chapter 55

Death would not come. Lily tried to give herself over to oblivion. The pain held her, pinned to the world, beating at her in waves and spasms and she couldn't make herself die.

Behind the lids of her eyes she saw Charlotte Mary, her hands outstretched. She saw her mother and father smiling, standing in the shadows, wavering and indistinct, but their essence was clear to her.

There were times when she was unaware, when the pain grew and grew until she cried out, until, in kindness, her failing body rescued her, plunging her deeper into the darkness. It was her goal, it beckoned to her, she wanted to go, to fall into the soft emptiness, but over and over it pushed her back, buoyed up on a wave of agony.

Charlotte Mary came again, she carried the little bundle with her, just as she had on the day the nightmare began. She held Peter towards her, only to snatch him back with a laugh and then open her arms to allow his tiny form to vanish into the ether.

Lily woke for an agonising moment, to find that in her stupor she was reaching out, her hands flexing, fingers clutching at the child that wasn't there. And then she tumbled back into the void.

It was cold and there was a moment when the pain had eased enough for her to think logically. She imagined climbing back up the stairs, up to her bedroom where she could wrap the warm duvet around her and stop shivering. If she could drag herself into the light, she could find some peace – she wanted, more than anything, to find some peace. She needed the toilet and panicked at the thought that she may well soil herself, and be found in a stinking pool. But then it didn't matter because the pain came back; it was all there was in the world, and she heard her voice from far away pleading for it to stop.

"No more, please, no more."

She saw the bright light. Didn't everyone say there was a bright light? Go into the light they said, and she tried, but didn't know how to do it.

When Terry spoke, she was confused. He wasn't part of them, the small phalanx of the dead, how was it that he was there? "Lily, Lily. Oh, bloody hell. Lily."

She opened her eyes to see his shape. A dark form behind the white glare of his phone torch. He knelt beside her. She could feel the warmth of him. He took off his jacket and laid it over her upper body. Such bliss, the warmth, the smell of his aftershave, the feel of his hand in hers. She moved her lips, but the sound she wanted to make would not come.

"Take it easy, Lily. We've called an ambulance. Sandra let me in with her key. You're going to be okay. What the hell are you doing down here? Why didn't you call for help? Oh shit, never mind about that. Why didn't you stay for the funeral? I was worried, you looked so ill. What are you doing here?"

He was gabbling – panicked and distressed. She forced her arm to move, clutched at his hand. She felt him rubbing at the skin, felt it move under his fingers. She raised the other arm and pointed to the corner of the cellar.

"Peter."

"What?"

"There. Take care of the baby."

Terry tried to calm the delirium. "He's alright, Lily, Peter's alright. We're going to take him and put him with his mum. When you're better. We'll go together. Don't worry about him now."

She managed to turn her head from side to side. "Letter. Read my letter. I'm sorry. I'm so sorry."

The next spasm of pain caused her to cry out and it spiralled, biting and vicious until it filled what there was left of the world.

"Lily, hang on, please just hang on. The ambulance will be here soon."

The warmth and ease was overwhelming, and as Charlotte Mary walked towards her, holding out the small bundle, darkness took her away, and the pain of it all dissipated like dew in the morning sun.

* * *

"Lily, aw shit. Lily." Terry watched the tension leave her body, saw her jaw loosen and fall. He turned to where her torch shone a cone of light into the corner. It lit the wall and on the dark floor there was the glint of glass.

He heard a siren, faint but growing nearer. The neighbour was calling from the kitchen, "They're coming. Tell her they're coming."

He called back to Sandra waiting upstairs, in the house, "I think it's too late, she's gone."

Then there was the clatter of feet along the hallway and down the wooden steps. He was pushed aside by the paramedics, but he knew it was too late. Still, she was old and sick. Probably it was a sort of release. He turned to leave but they asked him to wait.

When he told them what had happened, he made no reference to her peculiar final words. It would take too long to explain and it didn't matter anymore. She had kept his secrets and there was no need for them to become common property now.

After they had gone, and the police had asked their questions, taken his address, and Sandra had gone back to her own house, sniffling and shaking her head, Terry went back into the basement. Lily's torch still shone against the corner. He walked into the little pool of light. He frowned and bent to pick up the small vase holding a bunch of dying roses. There were a couple of candleholders, with metal night-light containers empty inside them.

It looked like a grave, or an altar. It made no sense. Perhaps they had buried a pet down here, a dog maybe or no, more likely a cat. Old spinsters, they all had cats – right? But why here, why not in the garden, up in the daylight?

He had assured Sandra that he would lock up and return the key, but first he'd just take a tour, ensure that everything was safe for the house to be left empty.

He went into the dining room and pulled open the door to the cabinet. He took out the blue jar. He could take it with him now, he wouldn't have to bother coming back. There was no point and he could keep his promise without too much trouble.

A second box stood alongside it. He carried them both to the table. 'Charlotte Mary'. Her name was on the label. A bit weird keeping all the ashes here in the cupboard. But then she must have had her reasons. Though he knew she had been kind and had tried to help him, he had thought that she was just a little odd.

The seals on the box were broken so he pried off the lid. There was a plastic bag inside containing a surprisingly small amount of ash. It had been sealed at some stage but someone had cut the top. The whole thing was very peculiar. Perhaps Lily had done something with a quantity of the ashes. Perhaps she had given them to someone. Did people do that?

He picked up the small blue urn and turned it in his fingers, it was heavy and when he shook it he could tell that it was full. The idea that crept into his mind was absurd.

Wasn't it?

Chapter 56

It was a bright, blowy day. The air was still warm, though the leaves were beginning to turn. Soon russet and gold would replace tired and dusty green. Their little convoy was alone in the cemetery. The air was alive with birdsong, and drying leaves rustled in a small breeze. Terry didn't come here often, his relationship with his mum had been such that he hadn't felt her loss in a way that drew him back, over and over, to be where her body lay. Granny had never been much more than a vague figure in his life. As for Clive, he had been true to his word: he had him cremated and his ashes scattered among many others in a rose garden in a different cemetery. He would never visit that place.

He had been here once already during the last couple of months though. He had brought flowers and stood for a while after he had laid them on the white pebbles. He hadn't spoken, there was no need as far as he was concerned. If there was anything of an afterlife with a connection to this one, then surely the dead, if they were still interested, were aware of anything they cared about. The time for conversation with them was long gone.

He held no grudge against the two women who were here. They had struggled as much as he. But the desperation to leave his past behind had robbed him of much affection for his maternal relatives, and there was no point looking for it here, in this place. He had visited to remind himself what it was like, just where he needed to come so it would be smooth and easy. He went away knowing that it would serve very well. It had been a pilgrimage of sorts, but he wasn't surprised to find that it left him unmoved. After years of subjugation, it took more than a stone in the ground and a rectangle of pebbles to stir his emotions.

The documentation had been easily done. He had help from all quarters and with the DNA results and the evidence from Lily's house, along with the letter she had left with her solicitor, the arrangements had gone surprisingly smoothly.

For him, the months since Lily had died had been a revelation.

Much of it was because of timing. There had been huge changes in attitude, and the publicity surrounding other children, other gangs of abusers, had caused a seismic shift in the way such things were handled. Nevertheless, the kindness he had encountered surprised him. The consideration he had been afforded eased the painful journey that he had thought he would never take.

People had listened to him, they had believed him, and then had offered him help to deal with the trauma of his past. He hadn't taken the help. He had already dealt with it in his own way. He had, after all, been fighting back since he was a child, on his own terms, and he was stronger every day.

He had refused all requests from the newspapers and television, for interviews and publicity. That wasn't for him. He didn't believe it would serve any purpose and had no desire to be in the spotlight.

They could do nothing about Clive. He had escaped real justice by dying so unexpectedly. But Andrew Stoner wasn't going to get away so easily. He had fled abroad, and the cause and circumstance of that sudden escape were still confused – although the reasons behind it were becoming clearer as more and more of his own victims came forward. No-one could understand how he had known that the truth was about to be revealed. There was a tentative connection with the buried child, which the newspapers had dubbed 'The Bone Baby' but the timing of his flight was a mystery. There had been online appeals, articles in the newspapers and fingers had pointed in surprising directions. Like a runaway truck, the thing had gathered speed and pace, and now seemed unstoppable. The dreadful coterie of the powerful and the rich had been outed and exposed. Terry had been warned that it could well be a couple of years before the investigations were complete. He was at ease with that.

When the time came, he would go to court – he would give what evidence there was, though in truth he didn't believe it was that much. Perhaps Clive had thought he was protecting his own family by keeping them to himself. Perhaps it had just been selfishness. There were others to whom he had not afforded such favour, and they were rising up now that the way was opened to them. Years of bullying and threats against the young and the vulnerable. So-called favours, in place of rental payments, yet more in the face of the threat of eviction.

The police gave Terry time and assured him that everything was a help and everything was examined. They pieced it together. He told them in detail about his own abuse. That had been the worst of it for him and yet, he had survived. The strongest evidence for his own case had been the DNA results, and in that his brother had been a witness as reliable as any long-suppressed stories of his own.

He had nothing but vague memories and dim facts about times when he was left in the car, or in downstairs rooms in rented houses. It became more meaningful when added to the other stories that were still being told.

He didn't meet the other victims. There was enough pain for him to carry without adding to it with that of strangers. Some of them were in touch with each other, with organisations that could offer care and counsel, but he didn't want that.

* * *

Today wasn't about himself, it was for his tiny, tragic family. He walked to the car parked behind his own with its rear door already opened.

The driver gave him an encouraging smile as he bent to lift the tiny white coffin. It wasn't heavy. He settled it safely in his arms and they walked together across the short grass to where Mum and Gran were waiting.

The small brass plate had just one name: 'Peter'. He had told them to leave off the surname, he didn't know what Lily had intended. The letter hadn't told them that. It didn't seem right to give him Clive's. They had his birthdate from the hospital card, but only an idea of exactly when he had died; again the letter was vague. It rambled about how short the time had been, and how painful it was.

Terry imagined that Lily had intended a meeting between them, a chance to tell her story in person, to explain why his brother had been in the cellar and why she had lied, why the pantomime with the ashes. In the end, she had tried to put things right. That was enough for him.

He had opted for nothing, rather than invent a convenient truth. The gravestone would be marked in the same way as this tiny casket, but he had instructed that it also bear the legend, 'Beloved Child'. It wasn't much but it seemed to him to be enough, and it was as genuine as anything else.

They had assured him that Peter's tiny body had been treated with kindness and respect. He thought Lily would have minded the disturbance, the examination, and felt sorry. But it was done now and the discovery had blown open the lid on secrets that she could never have imagined.

He hadn't looked at his brother's remains, there was no point. He hadn't known him, the sadness he felt was more for the circumstances than the child, and he felt no guilt either. His past had taught him that life was hard, and the only way through was to keep your eyes forward and to march on. He had come to terms with so much and convinced himself that he had been, always, an innocent victim.

He handed Peter over and stood silently as he was lowered into the ground. The sun shone on this part of the cemetery for a while each morning, and it was green and well-tended around the graves. As good a place as any to be left.

The driver of the hearse handed him a small bunch of flowers and he tossed them as gently as possible into the grave, and then he turned and walked away.

He had considered for a while that maybe he should bring Lily's ashes here and let her be with him. But she wasn't his family, so he had left that decision to Charlotte's nephew. He hadn't gone when they had taken them, with those of Charlotte Mary's from the house in Southsea, and scattered them on the waters of the Solent. He had no idea how the two women would have felt about that, but again, he didn't believe that the dead cared about such things. He had done the best that he could and he was moving on.

Once the authorities had finished their work in the basement, and ascertained that there were no other graves and that no crime had been committed in that house, except for the one sad, and relatively minor one, he had sold the Southsea property. It was too far away to be convenient and had needed a lot of refurbishment. For a while after he learned that Lily had left him almost everything, he had been unsure what to do. But she had done it freely, so he donated what he thought was a decent amount, in her name, to a children's charity. Later he was meeting with his accountant and a developer, to discuss the purchase of a new property in Bath city centre. It had promise.

Parts of Clive's will were still the subject of legal argument. There were bequests to people who were even now of interest to the police in the ring of criminals who had spoiled so many lives. They had told him, off the record, that it was entirely possible that he would keep the properties. It would be a sort of compensation they said. He hadn't answered, because he knew that there could be no such thing for a stolen childhood.

Andrew Stoner was refusing to help, denying knowledge of everything. It was probable they would extradite him from Spain, but it would all take time.

Many of the others who had been involved had accepted their fate and simply wanted as little fuss and attention as possible. The victims were determined that wouldn't be the case. It was a mess and would be difficult to sort out, but Terry had time, he had patience, and he had his revenge. As he drove out of the gates of Haycombe Cemetery, he lowered his car window and let the late summer breeze move the air around him.

It always seemed that it should rain at funerals, but today the sun seemed to be right – the warmth was a benediction.

The End

If you enjoyed this book, please let others know by leaving a quick review on Amazon. Also, if you spot anything untoward in the paperback, get in touch. We strive for the best quality and appreciate reader feedback.

editor@thebookfolks.com

www.thebookfolks.com

Printed in Great Britain
by Amazon

52756964R00147